THE CAGE

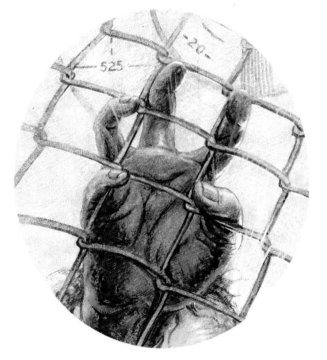

BRIAN KEENE

deadite
press

DEADITE PRESS
205 NE BRYANT
PORTLAND, OR 97211
www.DEADITEPRESS.com

AN ERASERHEAD PRESS COMPANY
www.ERASERHEADPRESS.com

ISBN: 1-62105-021-1

Printed in the USA.

Acknowledgements

For this Deadite Press edition of *The Cage*, my thanks to everyone at Deadite Press; Tod Clark and Mark 'Dezm' Sylva; Alan Clark; everyone at Cemetery Dance; everyone at Thunderstorm Books; Norman Prentiss; Keith Minnion; Steve Vernon, Tim Curran and Tim Lebbon; Mary SanGiovanni; and my sons.

This book is dedicated to Will Rogers, my old partner-in-crime… and my old partner in phony phone calls, as well. "Shake a hand, make a friend."

CONTENTS

THE
CAGE

ONE

The man barged through the door at 8:59 pm, just as they were locking up for the night. At first glance, Jeff Cusimano thought that the man must be a customer. But then, as he did with everyone who walked into Big Bill's Home Electronics, Jeff sized him up. Within seconds, he knew that the man wasn't there to buy a television or a stereo or a new computer. No. He was there for something else. This was something…different.

The man was dressed in black. Black shirt and black pants, both neatly ironed and pressed—the creases sharp. On his feet were black work boots, polished and un-scuffed. The store's fluorescent lights reflected off them. He wore a black knit cap on his head, as well as black sunglasses, even though it was nighttime and dark as shit outside.

The thing that really gave it away, though—the clearest indicator that the man wasn't there to buy a plasma screen television or a satellite radio—was the shotgun in his hands. It was black, too. Big and black. So was the large handgun holstered to the man's hip. The holster itself was also black. The knife strapped to his leg had a black hilt, although it couldn't really be called a knife, since the thick, angular blade was at least twelve inches long. No, Jeff decided, it wasn't a knife. It was a fucking machete. No sheath or anything—just bare, exposed steel. The neon lights of the store's sign out in the parking lot glinted off the blade—red, then blue, then red again.

Everyone stared, speechless, frozen in mid-task. Jeff stood behind the sales counter with Jared and Big Bill. Jeff had been totaling up the day's credit card receipts while Jared counted the cash in the drawer and filled out the bank deposit slip for the night drop. Big Bill had loomed over them both, loud and obnoxious and bloated, animatedly telling them how to do these tasks even though Jeff and Jared had done them hundreds of times before. Clint and Roy were lounging in the doorway that led into the backroom warehouse, smoking cigarettes and trying to decide what strip club to go to for the evening—The Odessa or the Foxy Lady (it was rumored that both establishments had ties to organized crime; The Odessa was supposedly run by the Russian mob, and the Foxy Lady was the last bastion of the dying, archaic Marano crime family, but for Clint and Roy, such rumors made patronizing the seedy clubs that much more exciting). Scott had been hanging out in the back of the store's showroom, standing next to the car stereo displays, cell phone to his ear, talking to his girlfriend, while Carlos walked the aisles, turning the televisions off one-by-one. That left Alan, who had been about to lock the door when the man barged in. As a result, Alan was closest to the intruder. Like the rest of his co-workers, he gaped. Unlike his co-workers, he spoke.

"I'm s-sorry, sir. W-we're closed." The keys jingled in Alan's shaking hand.

Jeff thought that in a surreal way, Alan's statement was sort of bizarrely comical. He wondered for a second if the man with the shotgun would say, "Oh, I'm terribly sorry about that. Please forgive me" and then just walk back out to the parking lot.

He didn't. Instead, the man let the glass doors slide shut behind him. He stared at Alan. Alan stared at him. A strange silence seemed to fill the store. Jeff held his breath. Then the intruder motioned at Alan with the barrel of the black shotgun.

"Lock the doors. Then give me the keys. Do anything else and you'll die."

His voice was perfunctory—his tone matter-of-fact. He spoke with an almost clinical detachment, as if the instructions he was giving Alan were the most boring, tedious thing in the world.

Alan didn't move, except for his trembling hands. He continued staring at the man with the gun. As Jeff and the others watched, Alan opened his mouth to speak, and then closed it again with a small moan. His eyes blinked rapidly.

"Do it." The man glanced away from Alan, quickly scanning the rest of the store. His demeanor was unperturbed.

Jump him, Jeff thought. *Now, while his attention is on us. He's not that big. You could take him, Alan. Get the shotgun and turn it on him. Or grab one of those pistols.*

Alan did none of this. Instead, he stuttered, "W-what?" A dark stain spread across the crotch of his khaki slacks. Even from behind the sales counter, Jeff could smell the sudden, pungent tang of piss. The keys continued to jingle in Alan's hand. Then the rest of him began to shake, as well.

Sighing, the intruder raised the shotgun, set the stock against his armpit and shoulder, and pulled the trigger. The weapon jumped in the gunman's hands. The explosion boomed across the store. In that split second, Alan seemed as surprised as everyone else. Then half of Alan's head disappeared. The pulped remains splattered all over the microwave oven display behind him. Jeff caught a glimpse inside Alan's head—teeth, nasal cavities, and the dripping gray and pink curds that were all that remained of his brain. Then Alan stumbled backward and slapped at a microwave with one flailing hand. His fingers slid across the buttons on the control panel, accidentally pressing them, and the unit hummed to life. The little light came on inside of the microwave, illuminating the blood dripping down the door. The turntable began to spin. Alan slid to the floor. Something slipped out of his head and splattered onto the carpet. His one remaining eye stared sightlessly. Blood jetted from him like water from a fountain, until his heart stopped. Then, the crimson flow became a trickle.

Jeff became aware that he was shouting, but he couldn't hear himself over the echoing blast. His ears rang as the sound of the gunshot faded.

Jared said, "What the fuck?" Jeff couldn't tell if his co-worker was screaming it, or merely mouthing the words.

The man in black moved quickly. He reached down, scooped up the key ring with one hand, and then turned his back on them. He checked the keys, one by one, searching for one that would fit in the lock. He seemed unconcerned that they might rush him or run away. In truth, Jeff didn't even consider it. He would have, just moments ago, but watching Alan's head blow up changed everything. Now, instead of fleeing, he just stood there behind the counter, stunned and numb, unable to act or to even think straight. His ears still rang, but he could hear again—at least partially. Jared stood next to him, screaming and pulling his hair. Big Bill still loomed behind them, but for once, the fat man was uncharacteristically silent. In an odd way, that seemed even more unreal to Jeff than Alan getting his head blown off. Still clutching his cell phone, Scott bent over and puked on the carpet. Carlos ducked down behind the television displays in an attempt to hide, but his loud wails and shrieks gave his location away. Roy and Clint dropped their still-lit cigarettes and fled into the warehouse. Jeff held his breath and watched them go.

The intruder grunted in satisfaction as a key slid into the lock. He turned it, locked the door, and then faced them again, dropping the keys into his pants pocket.

"I only need six," he said.

His voice was still unperturbed. Calm. The intruder projected an aura of confidence and self-assuredness that would have been almost soothing under different circumstances. To Jeff, he sounded like an accountant or a social worker. Jeff made his living by figuring people out. Selling them expensive televisions and surround sound systems was secondary. You couldn't close a sale until you knew your prey. You had to know what made them tick—had to know what methods would make them buy. A good salesman was nothing more than a student of people. Within two minutes of a customer walking into the store, Jeff could usually figure out what they did for a living, approximately how much they made per year, their marital status, and most importantly, whether they were in the store to pay or to motherfucking play. The gunman was single, or at least unmarried. There was no wedding band on his finger, and no white circle on the skin, left behind from where a ring would have been. His hair was neat. Not too short, but not too long, either. Professionally cut and styled. He had no facial hair, and his clean-shaven cheeks were free of five o'clock shadow. The intruder carried himself like a professional. He was efficient, no-nonsense, and very businesslike. Jeff guessed that he made over one-hundred thousand dollars a year.

Other than the guns, the knife, and the fact that he'd just blown Alan's head off, the man in black seemed totally normal—until the black sunglasses slid down his nose, and Jeff looked into his eyes. What he saw there chilled him. The man's eyes were dead and full of darkness. The man in black was definitely here to pay, rather than play. He was not fucking around. This was a no-nonsense individual. He knew what he wanted and he intended to get it. Jeff suddenly felt dizzy. The ringing in his ears—which had almost faded—grew louder again. His breath caught in his chest.

The intruder pushed the sunglasses back up on his nose and motioned with the shotgun barrel, pointing it at Scott, who was wiping puke from his lips with his tie.

"You. Get up here. Bring me the cell phone."

Scott made a noise like a squawking bird. The cell phone slipped from his fingers and clattered softly onto the gray-carpeted floor, narrowly missing the puddle of vomit.

"Pick it up," the man ordered. "Bring it up here, or you end up like your co-worker."

Groaning, Scott bent over, not taking his eyes off the intruder, and fumbled with the cell phone. He walked to the front of the store, head bowed, eyes on the carpet, holding the phone out in front of him like an offering to a god or king. He shuffled the last few feet and then stopped in front of the gunman. Scott glanced up. Jeff could see his Adam's apple bobbing up and down, although he wasn't speaking. When the man reached for the cell phone, Scott flinched.

"You call the cops?"

"No." Scott's voice was barely a whisper. "I was leaving my girlfriend a message when you walked in. It's her birthday today."

"It's more than that. Today is a very important day. The most important day of all."

"I…I don't understand."

"That's okay. You will. Did you tell her what was happening?"

Scott shook his head. "No, I had just hung up, before…"

He glanced at Alan's corpse and the rest of the sentence died in his throat.

The man flipped open the phone and after studying it for a moment, scrolled through Scott's text messages and list of calls. Regaining some of his bravery, Jeff mentally urged Scott to rush the intruder while he was distracted. Sure, the guy was armed, but he couldn't kill all of them at once, could he? If Scott would just be so kind as to possibly sacrifice himself, maybe the rest of them would get out of this alive. He wondered if Clint and Roy had gone out the back door. The warehouse was quiet—no sign they were still hiding back there. With luck, they were racing across the parking lot right now, calling 911 or shouting for help.

The man motioned with the shotgun again. "Everybody come out from behind the counter. Be quick about it. Line up over here, facing me. No talking. Remain still. Don't test me."

Jared made a squawking noise that reminded Jeff of a turkey. The two of them shuffled out from behind the counter, hands over their heads. Jeff's dizziness increased. He wobbled as he walked, and took deep breaths through his mouth. He felt his hands shaking above his head, and his pulse throbbed in his throat and temples. Nearby, Carlos crawled forward on his hands and knees, sobbing.

"And the two of you back there in the warehouse can come on out, too," the man shouted. "I know you didn't escape. I made sure of it before I came in. I blocked the rear exit and the loading door. You can't get out that way. No use hiding."

Roy and Clint tip-toed out of the back room, hands up in surrender. Their faces were pale and covered in sweat. Both men were older than the rest of their co-workers. Seeing their appearance, Jeff wondered if they were having heart attacks. Then sweat trickled into his eye, stinging it, and he realized that he probably looked as scared and disheveled as they did. "You too, fat boy." The killer pointed at Big Bill. "Get out here."

"Now look here," Big Bill hollered in what was his normal, blustery speaking voice—the voice he used to berate and badger customers into buying extended warranty service when they didn't want it. "I don't know who the hell you are, or what your major malfunction is, but that's enough of this nonsense. If you want money, we'll give it to you, but if you think we're—"

The shotgun was even louder the second time. Jeff closed his eyes to stop the room from spinning. He heard Scott puke again. Carlos and Jared screamed. Roy yelled something—it might have been "No" or "Oh." Jeff couldn't tell and didn't really care. When the shotgun blast faded, silence filled the store again—a noise-less vacuum shaped like Big Bill himself. Jeff opened his eyes.

Big Bill had been legendary among home electronics salesmen in Pennsylvania and Maryland. Over the years, he'd worked in all the usual places—Rex, Circuit City, Best Buy, Sears, American Appliance, and all the others. He'd been there when satellite television was brand new. He'd been there when projection screens were the next big thing, and when they became archaic, giving way to plasma and liquid crystal display. He'd even been there when compact discs made cassettes as extinct as eight-track tapes and vinyl. Big Bill had seen it all. He knew the trends. He knew the technology. Most importantly, he knew what people wanted and he knew how to sell it to them.

Eventually, he'd opened his own store, going toe-to-toe with the big box retailers in the area. Business had blossomed, despite the flagging economy. Bill knew the specs of every item in the store, and if he didn't know the specs, he'd bullshit his way through it, in order to make the sale. Big Bill was a closer. He was a pit bull, refusing to take no for an answer. He didn't give his customers a chance to think about it, or price shop else-where. Instead, he blitzed them with a bewildering barrage of technical data and price point information and flattery until they made a purchase just to escape him or shut him up. Big Bill liked to talk. If he wasn't twisting a customer's arm, then he jabbered at his employees, testing their product knowledge or giving them sales pointers. Big Bill was loud, obnoxious, and never laconic. He worked seven days a week, open to close, fueled on all-day combinations of coffee and energy pills and Red Bull. The store was his life. There was nobody waiting for him at home. Nothing to distract him on weekends. He had no hobbies or pets or loved ones. The only other things in Big Bill's life were an ex-wife and two kids who he never got to see because he was always working.

Despite all of his faults, Bill's employees respected him. Behind his back, they used to call him Bumble, after the creature from *Rudolph the Red-Nosed Reindeer*. The nickname had been apt, not only because Bill was large and loud, but because beneath it all, he had a good heart. He might piss them off throughout the day, but when push came to shove, he always had their backs, and he *always* took care of them.

And now he was dead, and his silence seemed strange and unfathomable to Jeff. It was hard to imagine not listening to Bill push an extended service plan on a customer ever again, or hear him breathing heavy on Friday mornings after unloading that week's deliveries from the truck, or berating Scott to "shake a hand and make a friend"—just one of his sales mantras. (Scott was always reluctant to approach customers when they first entered the store, preferring instead to give them time to look around for themselves before offering his assistance, and it had been a point of contention between the two.)

Jesus, Jeff thought. *Jesus Christ, this is really happening. This is really fucking happening.*

"Why did you do that?" Carlos sobbed. "Why would you fucking do that?"

The gunman shrugged. "I told you. I only need six."

"What does that mean?" A long strand of mucous dripped from Carlos's nose. "You're fucking crazy, puta."

"No," he whispered. "I'm not the crazy one. You are. All of you are. I'll show you. Just wait and see."

"L-look," Jeff stuttered, hating the fear and panic in his voice. "We don't want anymore trouble. Just—"

"Enough talking." With the barrel of the shotgun, the killer motioned to the warehouse door. "Let's go. Everyone into the back. No talking. Step out of line and I'll kill you all. And I'll do it slowly, because having to kill all of you would really piss me off. If that happened, then I'd have to do this all over again a year from now, and tonight would be a total loss. He doesn't want to wait a year."

Jeff felt a sick surge of jubilation. The guy wasn't making a lot of sense, but from what he was saying, it sounded like he might let the rest of them live, and Jeff desperately wanted to do that. But if so, then why had he insisted that he only needed six of them alive? What did that mean? For what purpose did he need them? Everything was happening so quickly. Jeff tried to sort it all out, but he couldn't decide what was happening. Was this a robbery, a hostage situation, or just some lone nut on a shooting spree? Or was it something else?

They marched single-file into the warehouse. Clint was in the lead. Their captor brought up the rear. They walked in silence, shoes scuffing the carpet, and none of them turned around to face the gunman. Jeff had never heard the store so quiet. Usually, the televisions and stereos were blaring. After all, you couldn't sell a high-end surround sound system unless the customer could experience its full power and potential right there in the store. But even when the units were turned off, there was still noise in the store—employees talking or a phone ringing. Now, it was utterly still.

Jeff glanced down and realized that they'd walked through Alan's blood. Red footprints marked their passage. When all of them were inside the warehouse, the killer

19

shut the door and ordered them to stop. Jeff stared up at the fluorescent lights and held his breath.

This is it, he thought. *If he's going to kill us, it will be back here. People will wonder where we are later tonight. Someone will report one of us missing. The cops will show up, and they'll find our bodies lying back here, bleeding out all over the concrete. Then we'll be on the news for a few days, until something else happens somewhere in the world. And that will be it. The end of our story.*

"Don't turn around. Don't talk. Just do as you're told. Empty all of your pockets. Everything. Cell phones, pagers, keys, money. Throw all of it on the floor. Now."

His voice was still calm, still matter-of-fact, as if he were asking about the difference between plasma and LCD screens or for an explanation of Dolby 5.1 and how to get the most from his center channel. Jeff felt like giggling at the absurdity of it all, but his will to live was stronger, and he suppressed the manic urge.

The group did as they were told. The warehouse rang with the sounds of coins and keys jingling, of cell phones cracking as they were dropped onto the hard concrete. Jeff went through his pockets, checking each item off his mental inventory as he cast it aside—his cell phone, his key ring, a handful of loose change, a small purple and black stone that he'd picked up from the sand during the vacation he and his ex-girlfriend, April, had taken to Ocean City, and finally, his money clip, which held his driver's license, credit card, debit card, health insurance card, and a few bills. The money clip was a graduation present from his parents. They'd bought it at the Things Remembered store across town—located in the same shopping mall where two of Big Bill's competitors were located. His initials were engraved on the money clip, along with his graduation date.

Jeff dropped all of his belongings on the floor one-by-one and stared straight ahead, biting his lip and trying not to shake. He heard the stone bounce off the floor and roll away. It felt like his life was rolling away with it. His thoughts turned to April. He wondered what she was doing now. He hadn't talked to her in months. Now, he might never talk to her again.

"Okay," the killer said. "Everybody take ten steps forward. Keep looking straight ahead."

Jeff shuffled along behind the others, silently counting his steps and expecting to hear the shotgun at any second. He wondered if he even *would* hear it. Wouldn't his head explode before the sound reached him? Did that happen with shotgun shells, or was it only with bullets? He didn't know. He focused on the drab, gray cement-block walls in an effort to distract himself from what was happening. Distraction seemed to offer some type of safety, no matter how fleeting, temporary, or false. His gaze flicked upward. Spider-webs dangled from the dusty ductwork overhead. The fluorescent lights hummed quietly. Above them, the shadows seemed to coil and twist. A few of the fluorescent bulbs had burned out. Jeff wondered if Big Bill had noticed yet, and if so, who would get the job of changing them—him, Jared or Alan. Usually the task fell to one of them, and they all hated it. Then Jeff remembered that both Alan and Big Bill were dead. It would have to be him or Jared, then. Maybe they could flip a coin to see who got to stand on the rickety ladder. The only fun part of the job was throwing the burned-out bulbs into the garbage dumpster behind the store, because they always exploded on impact. So, he and Jared had that to look forward to. All they had to do was stay alive.

The back room was filled with boxes of brand-new televisions, DVD and Blu-ray players, stereos, speakers, computers, printers, fax machines, microwave ovens, dishwashers, refrigerators, washers, dryers, video game consoles, dehumidifiers, entertainment centers, and more. They'd all been stacked neatly into rows, reaching from the floor almost to the ceiling. The ware-house was climate-controlled but a few of the boxes showed water damage from leaks in the roof. Big Bill had been talking about getting the roof patched, once the economy evened out. Now…

21

Jeff closed his eyes for a moment, afraid that he might fall over. When he opened them again, the logos on the boxes around him blurred. The warehouse seemed to be spinning. The ventilation system came on, rattling and blowing. Behind him, he heard what sounded like the intruder stomping on their cell phones and kicking their keys down the rows. Jeff clenched his fists, letting his fingernails dig into his palms, and bit down harder on his bottom lip. The pain brought him back into focus. He stared ahead again, trying desperately to keep his shit together.

At the far side of the warehouse was a loading door and a fire exit door. A basketball hoop without a net hung over the loading door, and an old dart board hung beneath that. A fire extinguisher occupied the wall between the two doors, along with a stand-up ashtray for Roy and Clint. Big Bill hadn't let them smoke in the store, but allowed them to do it in the back room. Usually, the two lurked in the doorway between the warehouse and the store, puffing away and watching for potential customers.

To the right of the fire exit was the employee restroom. The door to the restroom was slightly ajar, and both the light and the exhaust fan were on. Jeff caught a glimpse of the ugly pea-green walls, the cracked and smudged mirror, the filing cabinet full of various owners' manuals, recall notices, and warranty information, the dirty toilet, and the stack of old soft-core porno magazines and home electronics manufacturers' catalogs sitting on top of the toilet tank.

Next to the restroom was what they called the cage.

The cage was manufactured out of safety fencing and steel posts. Its length ran along most of the warehouse's rear wall, encompassing the space not occupied by the restroom or loading dock. One wall—the store's exterior wall—was composed of gray cement blocks. The other three walls, as well as the ceiling, consisted of the thick, stainless-steel wire fencing, as did the cage's padlocked door. Inside the cage were all of the store's small inventory—iPods, iPhones, Blackberrys, GPS units, digital cameras, camcorders, computer flash drives, and other items that were easy to steal. Most were stacked on shelves. Others were stacked on the floor, up against the wall. They kept the merchandise inside the cage as a security measure. Not that they'd ever had a problem with theft. Only Big Bill and Alan had keys to the cage. Anytime one of the employees sold an item housed inside of it, they had to get the keys from one of them. The store had over a dozen camcorders set up as security cameras. One of them was pointed directly at the cage.

"Okay," the man said, startling Jeff. "So far, so good. I'm going to frisk each of you, starting back here with you. What's your name?"

Jeff heard Roy moan, followed by a slapping sound.

"Your name, old man. What's your name?"

"R-roy…"

"Okay, good. Names are important. Knowing someone's name gives you power over them. Now, I'm going to start with Roy here. When I'm done, he's going to take these keys from me and unlock that security cage. He will go inside, followed by the next one and the next one. If any of you speak, or do anything other than proceed into the cage when it is your turn, you know what will happen. Do any of you wish to test me?"

No one responded.

"Good." Although Jeff couldn't see him, the man's tone sounded as if he was smiling. "Roy, you will leave the keys in the lock and leave the lock hanging from the door. When each of you enter the cage, you will move to the rear wall and stand there with your hands on it, with your backs to me. Do this, and I promise the evening will end well. Disobey, and it won't."

The ventilation system shut off again. The gunman fell silent. Jeff wondered what was happening, but resisted the urge to turn around and peek. A moment later, Roy brushed past him, head down, staring at the floor, Alan's key ring clutched tightly in one hand. His arms trembled as he unlocked the cage door and stepped inside, leaving the key in the padlock as ordered. He walked to the rear wall, put his hands over his head, and pressed his palms against the concrete blocks. He was followed by Carlos, then Scott, and then Jared. Jeff flinched as he felt the man's gloved hands on his buttocks. The search was quick but thorough. The killer's hands were strong and forceful. Jeff bit his lip until it was over. Then the intruder gave him a nudge forward.

Jeff walked past Clint, not daring to look back, and took his place next to the others. The concrete wall felt cold and rough beneath his fingertips. His stomach was in knots. He'd heard the expression before, but had never thought about what it meant until now. It felt like someone was twisting his intestines like pretzels. Jeff clenched his teeth, worried that at any second, he might shit his pants. His pulse throbbed, radiating from his chest to his throat to his temples. His face felt flushed, and even though the back room was cool, sweat poured down his forehead and back and arms.

Clint shuffled up next to him and placed his hands on the wall. Behind them, the cage door slammed shut. Jeff heard the hinged hasp fall into place, followed by the sound of the lock snapping shut. The keys jingled as their captor pocketed them.

"Okay, well done. See how easy that was? You can all relax now."

Slowly, Jeff turned around and faced the man. So did most of the others, except for Jared, who remained facing the wall and sniffling quietly.

"Now then." The man lowered the shotgun, pointing the barrel at the floor. "I've got things to do. Time is short."

Without another word, he turned around and strolled back out into the store, shutting the warehouse door behind him. Jeff, Jared, Clint, Roy, Scott, and Carlos all stared at the door and then gaped at each other in silence.

Then they all began talking at once.

"Jesus fucking Christ, what the…"

"I think I pissed myself…"

"This isn't happening…"

"Is he gone? Is he…"

"Shot Big Bill. Shot Big Bill and Alan…"

"Oh God, oh God, oh God…"

"Quiet." Jeff held up his hands. "Listen. Is he still out there?"

They fell silent and listened. Beyond the closed door, the intruder was whistling. The tune was familiar to Jeff, but he couldn't quite place it. Then they heard him begin to turn all of the televisions and surround sound systems back on. Alan and Carlos had turned them all off, as they did every night ten minutes before closing.

"What's he doing?" Scott whispered.

"Robbing the place," Clint said. "Duh."

Jared shuddered. "Let's just hope he hurries up and leaves after he gets what he came for."

"I don't think it's a robbery," Jeff said.

"Well," Carlos asked, "then what the hell do you think he's doing?"

"I don't know. But I don't think it's a robbery. Why would he waste time turning all of that shit back on, first of all? And if it was a robbery, then why didn't he take our wallets and stuff when he made us empty our pockets? Why didn't he empty out the cage? This is where the top-dollar stuff is, and it would be a lot easier to steal iPods and cell phones than to walk out of here with a big screen TV or a refrigerator."

"What about the cash drawer," Roy suggested. "Maybe he just wants that?"

"Maybe." Jeff nodded. "But then why not just ask for it at the beginning? Why herd us all back here and go through all of that? If he just wanted the cash, why waste all that time? And besides…"

His voice trailed off as he listened to the sounds from out in the store grow louder. It sounded as if the intruder had turned up every television and stereo full blast.

Carlos nudged him. "Besides what, Jeff?"

"He…he said he only needed six."

"Yeah." Roy shook his finger at the others. "I caught that too. Weird shit. What the hell did he mean by it?"

"I thought it meant that he needed six of us alive," Jeff said.

"I heard him, too," Jared whispered, "but I thought he was talking about money. I thought maybe he needed six hundred dollars or something."

Despite the tension inside the cage, Jeff grinned at that. He noticed that Roy was grinning, too.

"On a Thursday night? In this frigging economy? With everybody either wanting to put things on layaway, or just having us explain all the technical aspects to them so that they can turn around and buy it at Wal-Mart for half price? Fat chance. We won't have that much cash on hand until the weekend."

"But a robber wouldn't know that," Jared insisted. "And Bumble offered him money, right...right before he got shot."

They all fell silent for a moment. Then Scott shook his head.

"If it's a robbery," he said, "then why is the sick fuck turning the volume up on all the televisions and stuff?"

Jeff thought about pointing out that he'd already mentioned this, but didn't. Scott was scared. They all were scared. Last thing any of them needed to do right now was start breaking balls.

"To mask the sound," Carlos answered. "That way, nobody hears him. All they hear is the televisions and shit."

"If he was worried about noise," Jeff said, "then he wouldn't have shot Alan and Bill." Jeff couldn't bring himself to refer to his dead boss by the man's nickname. Calling him Bumble now seemed wrong somehow. "That fucking shotgun was a lot louder than anything else in this store. And besides, who's going to hear him, anyway? The parking lot is empty, except for our cars."

"Shit," Clint muttered. "We're all alone in here. I mean, nobody is gonna notice I'm missing, except for my dog. I don't get my kids until next weekend."

"I told my wife that me and you were going out after work," Roy replied. "So she won't miss me until after midnight. What about the rest of you?"

"I was leaving my girlfriend a message on her voicemail," Scott said, "right before he came in. She's expecting me later tonight. I was going to take her out for her birthday."

"Okay, that's good!" Roy's expression grew excited. "What time is she expecting you?"

"Not until eleven. She had to work late at the hospital. We were going to hit Fat Daddy's. Last call isn't until one."

"Shit. Eleven o'clock. That's two hours from now." Roy turned to Carlos, Jared and Jeff. "What about you guys?"

Carlos shrugged. "I got nobody, man. My girl moved out three months ago. Been living alone ever since. Nobody's expecting me."

Jared nodded. "Me neither."

Jeff just shook his head.

"Well," Roy's eager expression turned to defeat, "then that's that, I guess. We're screwed."

The cacophony from the store grew even louder. Jeff listened to competing noise. Subwoofers rumbled with explosions from *The Dark Knight*. Surround sound systems blasted a battle scene from *Independence Day* (while dated, the movie still provided an outstanding display of home theatre's full potential). CNN's Campbell Brown read the news simultaneously from twenty different televisions. Circle of Fear, Vertigo Sun, Lupara, Fergie, and Redman competed for stereo supremacy in the store's audio section. The noise reached a confusing, maddening level. Then the warehouse door opened and the sounds grew even louder, blasting into the room with enough force to make Jeff wince.

The intruder strolled up to the cage and tapped on the wire. Jeff noticed that he no longer had the shotgun or the machete, and assumed that he'd left the weapons lying somewhere in the store. The handguns were still holstered at the killer's sides.

"You're on satellite dish here?"

Jeff had to strain to hear him over the crush of sound. When none of them answered him, the man un-holstered his pistol and raised it to chest level. He tapped the barrel against the cage.

"Answer me, or I'll shoot one of you in the gut or the knee. Doesn't matter to me, and it takes a very long time to die from such a wound. Time enough for me to finish."

"Yes," Carlos said, raising his voice to be heard over the noise. "We're on satellite dish. We sell them, and having the televisions hooked to it makes it easier to demonstrate. And some of the televisions have DVD and Blu-ray players hooked up to them, too."

"And the audio section? Is that satellite radio?"

Carlos nodded. "That, along with iPods and compact discs."

"What about Wi-fi? Do you have that here?"

"No," Carlos said. "The bookstore down the street has it, but it doesn't reach this far."

With his free hands, the man pulled the keys from his pocket.

"What's your name?"

"C-Carlos..."

"Okay, Carlos. I want you to show me. The rest of you stand back against the wall until Carlos leaves."

His eyes didn't stray from them as he unlocked the cage and opened the door with one hand. He kept the handgun trained on them with his other hand.

"Come on," he said. "Let's go."

Carlos didn't move. "You...you're not gonna kill me, are you? I've done everything you asked."

"I want you to show me how to turn the satellite off. Then I want you to switch all of the televisions over to broadcast, and the audio over to AM."

"S-sir...there's nothing on the broadcast channels anymore. Everything has converted over to digital."

"I know. That's why we're doing this. Digital broadcast is no good."

28

"And I don't know if we can get AM radio in here."
Carlos's tone was apologetic and plaintive. "There's no
antennae. And with these thick walls, we won't pick up any
signals. All you'll hear is static."

"All I *want* is static. And all I want from the televisions
is an empty broadcast channel. I want no signal, whatsoever.
No signal from the televisions. No signal from the stereos.
No signal from anything. Understand?"

Carlos nodded. Jeff saw the confusion in his eyes. It
mirrored his own.

"Good." The man motioned with the pistol. "What's
your name, again?"

"Carlos."

"That's right. Excellent. That's a good name. Full of
power. Now, come on, Carlos."

Carlos shuffled out of the cage. The man placed the pistol
barrel against his head, and then closed and locked the cage.
Then he turned back to the others.

"Remember. That security camera is watching everything
you do. That means I'm watching, too. I found your little
security monitors behind the sales counter. Don't get any
ideas. Work with me, and this will all be over soon."

He marched Carlos out of the warehouse. As they left, he
began humming the same tune Jeff had heard him whistling
earlier. Jeff still wasn't able to identify it. As they walked
through the door, the gunman stopped humming and sang a
snatch of lyric.

"You don't have to be a Shtar, baby, to be in my show."

Then he began humming again. He guided Carlos through
the door and out into the store. The door closed behind them,
and the noise from the televisions and stereos settled back
down to a dull roar.

"Well," Clint muttered. "That right there just proves how
crazy he really is."

Roy nodded. "I would have never guessed that guy was
a fan of Marilyn McCoo and Billy Davis Jr."

"What?" Jeff frowned. "Who are they?"

Roy shook his head sadly. "You kids. If it's not Guns n Roses, you don't know about it."

"I was six years old when Guns n Roses came out, Roy. *Appetite For Destruction* was the first cassette I ever bought. How about you get with the times? Guns n Roses are classic rock, now."

"Well, even still…"

Jeff rolled his eyes. "Who are Billy Davis and Marilyn Mc-whatever?"

"I know," Scott said. "Billy Davis is the guy who played Lando in *Empire Strikes Back* and *Return of the Jedi*."

Clint groaned. "That's Billy Dee Williams, you dip-shit. Billy Davis and Marilyn McCoo were one-hit wonders in the Seventies—back when Roy and I were your age and dinosaurs still walked the fucking Earth."

Jeff snapped his fingers. "You don't have to be a star, baby, to be in my show!"

Roy nodded. "That's it. That's the song he was humming."

"But that's not what he said."

"What do you mean?"

"He sang something else. The words were a little different. He didn't say star." Jeff frowned, trying to remember. "Scar? Spar? Shtar?"

"I think it was Shtar," Scott said.

"Yeah," Jeff agreed. "That was it."

"So not only is he crazy," Clint said. "He's got a speech impediment, too."

The noise from the store continued for another minute. Then it began to slowly fade.

"Carlos must be switching everything over for him," Roy said.

The others nodded. They waited for Carlos to return, but he didn't. There were no gunshots. No screams or shouts. The store was silent.

They waited, wondering what time it was, wondering if anyone would find them, and wondering what was happening out beyond the cage.

TWO

"I've got to piss."

Clint shifted from one foot to the other, looking miserable. His expression was pinched and pained. He clutched his groin with one hand. Nobody answered him. The only other sounds in the cage were Jared's quiet, muffled sobs. He'd started crying again soon after the gunman had departed with Carlos. Jared had collapsed in the corner, sitting with his back against a stack of cell phones, knees drawn up to his chest, arms wrapped around his legs, face hidden, sobbing. He'd been unresponsive to all of their attempts to console him. Eventually, they'd just left him alone.

"He said something else," Jeff told them. "Before. I just thought of it now. He said that he doesn't want to wait a year. Not him, meaning the gunman. It sounded like he meant someone else."

Scott nodded. "Yeah, I caught that, too. Maybe he's got a partner outside in a getaway car?"

"Or maybe he's just crazy," Roy said.

"I've *really* got to piss," Clint repeated, squeezing his crotch. "My back teeth are floating."

"Hold it," Jeff said.

"I don't think I can. My eyes are turning yellow."

"Well, for Christ's sake, don't do it in here! We're in enough shit without it smelling like a toilet in here, too."

"Oh, fuck off, Jeff. You always were Bumble's little pet."

Jeff whirled around and advanced on the older man. "Really? We've been locked up for ten minutes. Are we really going to start turning on each other already, Clint? Is that how you want this to go? Like every hostage movie ever made?"

Clint held up his hands in surrender. "You're right. I'm sorry. I'm just…scared."

"We all are," Jeff said. "It's cool. I'm sorry, too."

"I really *do* need to piss, though. Whatever he's doing out there, I hope he lets us out of here soon."

"*If* he lets us out." Scott gripped the wire cage with both hands and stared out into the warehouse. "They've been gone a long time. Maybe he's left already. Killed Carlos and then high-tailed it the fuck out of here."

"Stop it," Roy said. "That line of thinking will lead to no good. He didn't kill Carlos. He said that he wouldn't."

"No," Scott replied. "That wasn't it. All he said was that he needed six of us."

"Same thing."

"Maybe," Jeff said. "Or maybe not. Even if it is, how can we believe him? I mean, I don't know about you, Roy, but I kind of have a hard time taking the word of some crazy fucker who just blew away two of my friends. You said yourself he might be nuts."

"Exactly." Scott nodded in agreement. "And he never said that he wasn't going to kill us. Carlos asked him point blank, and all he said was that bullshit about the satellite signals."

"I don't know," Roy said. "If he was going to kill us, I would think he'd have done it when he marched us back here. Or once he'd locked us inside. Why draw it out?"

None of them answered.

"I wish he hadn't taken our cell phones," Clint said.

"Why?" Jeff wrapped his fingers around the cage's wire mesh and stared out into the warehouse. "It wouldn't have mattered anyway. There's too much concrete back here. We wouldn't have been able to get a signal."

"Then why did he smash them?"

Jeff shrugged. "Maybe he didn't know that. Or maybe he just wanted to make sure."

Scott scratched his chin thoughtfully. "He did say that he didn't want anything sending out or receiving a signal. Maybe that meant our cell phones, too."

"No," Roy said. "That wasn't it. He said something about—"

Jeff interrupted them both. "Guys, we're debating the ravings of a nutcase here. I mean, come on. Does it really matter what he said or what he didn't say? The guy is a fucking loon. We're looking for logic where there is none. Rational people don't walk into stores and start shooting the employees. He's crazy. End of story. Instead of worrying about his manifesto, let's concentrate on getting the hell out of here."

Jared stirred from his spot on the floor and looked up at them. Tears and snot covered his face.

"That's a great idea, Jeff." Spittle flew from his lips as he spoke. His voice was thick and hoarse with sarcasm and panic. "I'm glad you're in charge!"

"What's your problem?"

"My problem? Well, first of all, how do you suggest we escape? In case you haven't noticed, we're locked up in the fucking cage!"

Jeff opened his mouth to respond, but then paused. The fact was, he hadn't the faintest idea how to escape. He hadn't thought about it until now.

"I don't know," he admitted. "I've been too preoccupied with thinking that I was going to be shot."

They all fell silent for a moment. Jared slowly clambered to his feet and wiped his eyes and nose with the sleeve of his white dress shirt. He sniffed a few more times. Then he stared down at the floor.

"Sorry," he mumbled, not looking up at them. "Sorry I freaked out."

"It's okay," Jeff told him, softening his voice. "Don't worry about it. Like I told Clint, we're all scared. We just need to hold it together—come up with a plan. I don't want to die tonight, and I'm pretty sure the rest of you don't either."

"I'm gonna die if I don't piss soon," Clint groaned. "It really frigging hurts."

"Hang in there," Roy told him.

"That's easy for you to say. You don't have an enlarged prostate."

Roy grinned. "Yeah, but my liver is trying to kill me. Want to trade?"

"Hell, no." Clint smiled in response, despite his clear discomfort. "I happen to know that in addition to your liver, you can't get it up anymore. I don't need those problems."

"Who told you that?"

"Your wife."

"Could we pry the fencing up?" Scott asked, interrupting their banter. "Maybe wedge something under it and lift a section far enough off the floor that Jared could crawl out?"

"W-why me?" Jared stammered, his eyes suddenly wide. "I don't want to go out there with that guy on the loose. What if he catches me?"

"You're the skinniest," Scott explained. "I don't think Jeff or I could fit underneath it, and there's no way in hell that Clint or Roy would."

"Thanks," Roy said. "I appreciate that. Nothing like being told you're fat right after your best friend tells everyone you can't get it up, either."

Scott motioned to the wire mesh. "You want to try it? Be my guest."

"No thanks." Roy shook his head. "It wouldn't work, anyway. I mean, it's a good plan, but we wouldn't be able to bend or lift the wire high enough. There's too much tension between the poles. That mesh is tighter than a Catholic school virgin. They manufacture it that way to prevent theft."

"Too bad they didn't manufacture it with an escape route, too," Jeff said. "Didn't they ever plan on people getting accidentally locked inside?"

"Watching the security camera," he whispered. "And wondering if he's watching us."

The others paused.

"Oh shit," Jeff said. "I forgot about that."

"Fuck him," Scott snarled. "I don't care if he is watching. We can't just sit here and wait. We've got to do something."

He began rummaging through the box. After a moment, Jeff and Roy joined him. They searched through the miscellaneous junk—spare belts and bags for the store's vacuum cleaner, remote controls for floor-model televisions that they no longer had in stock, assorted batteries, instruction manuals for various electronics, a black magic marker, paper clips, audio patch cords and cables, a pack of matches from the Odessa, and a camcorder charger for a model that had been discontinued years before. There was nothing useful—nothing that they could use as a tool or a weapon. Frustrated, they each stood up again.

Clint whimpered softly.

"Hang in there," Roy told him again.

Scott sighed. "We're fucked."

"We're not fucked," Jeff said. "Don't start thinking like that. We've got to stay positive."

Scott rolled his eyes. "Yeah, because *that* will keep us safe."

"Maybe he's out there laughing at us," Jared said, his gaze still focused on the camera. "Maybe this is how he gets his jollies. I hope Carlos is okay. I wonder what he's doing with him?"

"Don't think about it," Jeff advised. "I know that sounds cold, but that's how it is. There's nothing we can do for Carlos until we figure a way out of here."

If Jared heard him, he gave no indication. He continued staring straight ahead, and his voice was low, as if he was talking to himself. "I liked Carlos. He was nice. If a customer came in on my day off, and they'd been working with me before, and he rang up the sale, he always entered it in the computer under my name, so I'd get the commission. The rest of you never did that. You'd always ring it up as a split."

"Jared," Scott said, "we need to focus on more important things right now."

Jared turned around. His shoulders were slumped and his expression was sullen.

Clint moaned again. His face was pale, and beads of sweat rolled down his forehead. He clenched his jaw so hard that Jeff could hear his teeth grinding against each other.

"I've got an idea," Roy said quietly. He bent over and rummaged through the junk box again until he found the matchbook. "These are probably mine. You guys remember when Sikes worked here?"

Jeff and Scott nodded. Jared frowned and then shook his head.

"You wouldn't remember him, Jared. He was fired long before you got hired. Sikes was a real dirt bag. Bumble hired him during the Christmas rush one year. He dressed like a slob, came in drunk all the time or reeking of marijuana, had the manners and personality of a rock, and couldn't sell shit to save his life. But that wasn't why he got fired."

"He was a thief," Jeff said. "Used to steal people's lunches right out of the fridge."

Roy nodded. "And then we caught him trying to swipe a VCR out of the back. He'd put it in with the trash and hauled it outside, then hid it behind the dumpster. Clint happened to be sitting in his car at the time, hung over, and saw him do it."

"Piece of shit," Clint said. Scott grinned. "I remember that. Bill went fucking nuclear, man. He really did look like the Bumble from Rudolph when he hollered at Sikes."

"I thought for sure he'd punch Sikes," Jeff agreed. "Or have a heart attack restraining himself from punching him."

"Clint and I had been hiding our cigarettes back here," Roy said. "Remember, Bumble didn't like us having them in our shirt pockets while we talked to customers? He thought it looked unprofessional. But we couldn't just leave them lying around either, because Sikes would fucking steal them. So we hid them back here in the cage."

Roy stared at the matchbook, and seemed lost in thought. A slight, sad smile crossed his face. Jeff put a hand on the older man's shoulder and gently squeezed.

"You said you had an idea?"

Roy glanced up at him, and Jeff was surprised to see that his eyes glistened with tears. Sniffling, Roy smiled again and then stood up. His knees popped loud enough for the others to hear them.

"Yeah." He pointed beyond the wire mesh, towards the

ceiling. "I've got an idea. You guys see the sprinklers? What if we start a fire? It doesn't have to be a big fire. Just enough to get some smoke up there around the ceiling. Then the sensors will detect it and the sprinklers will kick on."

"Holy shit," Scott gasped. "You're right! The system will automatically alert the fire department when the sprinklers come on."

"Exactly," Roy said, holding the matchbook up triumphantly.

"It won't work," Clint said. He leaned against the shelves with his legs crossed. "Remember? Bumble told us that it was heat that set the system off. Not smoke. Otherwise, we wouldn't have been allowed to smoke cigarettes back here."

"Shit," Jeff and Scott said in unison.

Roy didn't respond. He lowered the matchbook. His smile vanished. His expression crumpled. His bottom lip began to quiver. Then, he began to weep silently. Tears spread out around the crow's feet next to his eyes and rolled down his cheeks.

"It will be okay," Jeff said. "It was a good idea, Roy. Take it easy. We'll think of something else."

"What if we just made a fire big enough to produce some heat?" Scott asked. "The sensors will detect that, too. Right?"

Clint shrugged. "Yeah, I think so. But it's got to be really hot."

"Well," Scott continued, "we can do that. I mean, we've got all these iPod and cell phone boxes in here with us. We could use them as fuel. Wouldn't that work?"

"We're in a small, confined space," Jeff reminded him. "We'd be toast before the fire got hot enough."

The ventilation system kicked on again. Jared, Clint and Roy jumped at the sudden sound. Clint yelped.

"Guys," he moaned. "I'm sorry. I just can't hold it anymore. I've *got* to piss…right now. My fucking bladder is going to explode if I don't."

Jeff sighed. "Do us one favor, okay?"

"What's that?"

"Stick it out through the cage, at least? Piss out there, rather than in here."

Nodding, Clint limped towards the wire mesh. He unzipped his fly and shuddered. The others turned away to give him privacy. Before he could begin, however, the door opened again and the killer walked back into the warehouse. All of them turned back around and stared at him in silence and fear. Clint gaped, his hands wrapped around his flaccid penis, the tip of which was still sticking through the mesh. Then he groaned, long and loud. The gunman glanced down at his penis and arched an eyebrow.

"You need to go that bad?"

Clint nodded dumbly.

"Okay." The intruder shrugged. "Come on, then. Let's get you taken care of."

He raised the pistol and pointed it at them as he unlocked the cage.

"Each of you step to the back."

They did as commanded. The hinges creaked as the door swung open. Jeff noticed that again, not only was the shotgun missing, but the machete was missing, as well. The killer was still armed only with the pistol.

"Come on," the man in black urged Clint. "I don't have all night. Things to do. Time is short. He's waiting."

Clint glanced back at his friends. He blinked rapidly. Then he zipped up his pants and shuffled forward, wincing in pain and discomfort with each step. Their tormenter snickered at him. Clint's cheeks turned red. He hung his head.

"You weren't kidding," the gunman said. "You really do need to go."

"Yeah..."

He motioned Clint aside with the handgun. Then he locked the cage door again, and led Clint forward. Clint paused when they reached the restroom door, but the gunman poked him between the shoulder blades with the pistol's barrel.

"Nope. Not here. Keep going out into the store."

"But…I have to pee really bad."

"I know. You can do it out in the store."

He prodded him with the gun again, and Clint stumbled forward. Jeff, Roy, Jared and Scott watched them leave. The warehouse door swung shut. Silence returned. Scott summed up what they were all thinking. "Shit. What do we do now?"

"What else can we do?" Jeff replied. "We wait."

THREE

"We should have rushed him when the cage was still open," Jeff said. "Damn it!"

"So why didn't you?" Jared mumbled.

"Because everything happened so quickly. I just wasn't thinking."

"He'd have shot us if we'd tried anything," Roy said.

"Would he have? I don't know, dude. I kept thinking about it when he first came into the store. If Alan or somebody had rushed him at the start, maybe we wouldn't be in here right now."

"Or maybe they'd still be dead and so would we," Roy countered. "I much prefer being locked inside the cage."

"Speak for yourself," Jeff replied.

Roy arched an eyebrow in surprise. "You're saying that you'd rather be dead than locked up?"

"No, I'm saying that I'd rather be the hell out of here. And did you guys notice? When he took Clint, he made mention of a partner again. He said somebody was waiting."

"I think he meant Carlos," Jared said.

Jeff and Roy glanced at each other, but neither of them replied.

"I hope they're okay." Jared sighed.

Jeff, Roy and Jared were seated on the cold concrete floor. Scott paced the cage in an endless loop, hands stuffed in his pockets, face pinched with concentration. Roy held out a hand and stopped him on his next pass.

"Why not sit down?" he asked. "You might as well save your strength. Walking in circles won't do any good."

"You don't understand," Scott said. "I can't just sit here and do nothing."

"And pacing back and forth is accomplishing what, exactly?"

Scott shrugged. "I don't know. It's keeping my mind busy, at least. I've been thinking about Amanda. When I saw her this morning, we only had a few minutes. I told her that I loved her and gave her a kiss—a peck on the cheek, but that was all. And I didn't really mean it, you know? I told her that I loved her but I didn't really think about the words. It's just something you say—force of habit. I want her to know that I meant it."

"You'll get the chance," Roy said. "Have faith."

"I'm supposed to pick her up at eleven. Anybody know what time it is?"

"He took our watches," Jeff reminded him, "but I'm guessing we've been in here at least an hour. Maybe longer."

"No," Roy said. "More like half an hour. Forty minutes, tops."

"How can you tell?" Jeff asked.

Roy sighed. "By the strength of my nicotine fit. If I go more than half an hour without a cigarette, my mouth gets dry and I start to get really bad headaches right behind my eyes, and right now, it feels like somebody is shoving a knife into my forehead and my mouth feels like sandpaper."

"Where were you meeting Amanda?" Jared asked Scott.

"I'm supposed to pick her up at the hospital when she gets done working. If I'm late, she'll call my cell phone."

"And when you don't answer?" Jeff asked. "What will she do then?"

"I don't know. She might call here looking for me, I guess."

"Will she worry?" Roy asked. "If you're not there to pick her up right away?"

Scott began pacing again. His shoes made scuffing sounds on the concrete floor. "Not immediately, no. But she'll start freaking out if she can't track me down. It's her birthday, after all. She knows I wouldn't stand her up."

Roy pressed him. "So what do you think Amanda will do? Would she call the police or the hospitals? Call your friends?"

"Eventually," Scott said. "She'd probably try my cell a few times. Then the store. Then our friends."

Roy crossed his fingers. "Let's hope so."

Jeff frowned. "She wouldn't try to come here, would she?"

"Oh shit!" Scott stopped in mid-step and smacked his forehead with his palm. "I didn't think about that. Fuck!"

Roy, Jared and Jeff stared at him. Scott's eyes grew wider. He moved his hand from his forehead to his mouth.

"If she shows up here, she'll see that my car is still in the parking lot. That means she'll knock on the door. At the very least, she'll peek through the glass—try to see if I'm in here. If that crazy fucker sees her…oh my God! I've got to get out of here. I've got to…if Amanda…"

He whirled around, crossed the floor in two quick strides, and gripped the chain links.

"Hey," Scott hollered. "Hey, you out there! You've got to let us out of here. You can't just hold us like this. You've got to—"

Jeff leapt to his feet and grabbed Scott by the shoulders, pulling him away from the fencing. Scott resisted, clutching the wire mesh with both hands. The chain links rattled and jingled. Scott was hyperventilating, and his breathing echoed throughout the warehouse.

"Chill out," Jeff said. "Damn it, Scott, calm down. Don't give the fucker the satisfaction of knowing that you're scared."

"Jesus Christ," Scott sighed. "Jesus fucking Christ. Amanda, dude! Amanda…"

Jeff guided him to the center of the cage and gently forced him to sit down. Scott's breathing was still rapid and loud.

"She'll be okay," Roy offered. "It's not even eleven yet. It will be a long time before Amanda begins to worry."

"Roy's right," Jeff said. "Let's just stay calm and figure this shit out. No reason to give him a show over that security camera."

"I don't think he's watching," Jared said.

"Why?" Jeff asked. "You seemed convinced that he was earlier."

"When he came in the last time, he didn't mention anything about you guys going through the junk box. If he'd seen that, I would think he'd have been in here right away, or at least commented on it."

"Maybe he saw that we didn't find anything useful," Jeff said.

"He seemed surprised when he saw Clint getting ready to piss," Roy pointed out. "If he was watching us on the camera, you would think he'd have noticed how Clint was standing. He was holding his dick and practically hopping up and down on one foot."

"The gunman's probably been too busy with Carlos," Jared suggested. "And with Clint, now. Too busy to watch the cameras."

None of them replied. Jared's words seemed to hang in the air. The ventilation system rattled to life again. They sat in silence, each man lost in his own thoughts until it kicked off once more. Finally, Jeff stirred.

"It's awfully quiet out there. I haven't heard Carlos or Clint or…anything."

"They're okay," Roy said. "They have to be."

Jeff nodded without much conviction. Jared covered his mouth with his hand, sneezed, and then wiped his palm on his pants. Scott stared straight ahead, arms wrapped around his knees as he rocked slowly back and forth.

"Clint's been in worse situations than this," Roy said, grinning. "Hell, we both have. Many times. You guys ever hear about the time we almost got arrested at American Appliance?"

"I don't think so," Jeff said.

"It was before any of you guys worked here, right after Bumble…Bill, opened the store. Clint and I used to be the ones who had to go around to all of the competitors' stores once a week and price shop. These days, that's Alan's job."

It was, Jeff thought. *But I don't think he'll be doing it anymore.*

"Anyway," Roy continued, "me and Clint were in

American Appliance one day. We were dressed down so that we wouldn't stick out like salesmen. We had our little notebooks with us, so we could jot down model numbers and prices, and then come back here and make sure our store stock was marked down to beat their prices. Anyway, Clint used to like to fuck with the other salesmen. He'd tie them up for thirty or forty minutes, keep them busy pretending that he was shopping for a big screen or a home theatre system—run them through all their paces, and then of course walk out without buying anything. The theory was that real customers would get tired of waiting and come to our store instead."

"Pretty slick," Jeff said.

"It was. But that day, he picked the wrong salesman to mess with. Turned out, the guy knew who we were because he'd been price-shopping our store. He recognized us right away, but he toyed with Clint for a little bit. The guy kept telling Clint that he should buy it there, rather than at Big Bill's Home Electronics, because all of the salesmen at Big Bill's were crooks—especially a guy named Clint. He kept saying stuff like that. Clint got pissed off. The tips of his ears were red, he was so mad. And then the guy told him that he knew who Clint was, and to get the fuck out of the store. Well, that didn't sit well with Clint."

"What happened?" Scott asked.

"Clint took a swing at him. Knocked the guy backward into a fifty-two inch Panasonic projection screen. I dragged Clint out of there but not before their manager called the cops. Luckily, they didn't press charges."

Jeff and Scott laughed. Jared smiled. "Crazy bastards," Scott said.

Pausing, Roy smiled. "Clint used to do things like that all the time. I can't tell you how many strip clubs and bars I've pulled him out of before he could get in a fight. And now…"

His smile faded. His bottom lip trembled.

"And now he's out there and I'm in here and there's nothing I can do to help him…I can't pull him out."

"Hey," Jeff said. "Don't think about it that way, Roy.

Like you said, he's been in bad situations before. If anyone can talk their way out of a jam, it's Clint. Besides, if the crazy dude had killed Carlos or Clint, we'd have heard the gunshots. We haven't. It's been quiet. Chances are good that they're still alive. He said he needed the six of us."

"Then what's he doing with them?" Jared asked. "He's been out there too long for this to be a robbery."

"I don't know," Jeff replied. "Maybe he did have a partner. Maybe they pulled a box truck up to the front door or something, and he's making them help him load up stuff—all the floor models and display units."

"But if they were doing that, then we'd hear them."

"Not necessarily," Scott said. "We can't hear shit when that ventilation system is running. Maybe most of the noise happened while it was on."

"They're not dead," Roy insisted. "Jeff is right. They can't be dead."

"But how do you know for sure?" Jared asked.

"Because they just can't. Now let's just focus and try to stay positive, okay?"

Scott snickered. The others glanced at him.

"What's so funny?" Roy asked.

"Sorry. I was just…it's weird, the shit your mind turns to in a situation like this."

"What were you thinking about?" Jeff asked.

"Fuck Around Quotient Zero. You guys remember that?"

They nodded, and Jeff laughed. On slow weekdays—days when the store averaged less than a dozen customers from open to close—the salesmen did things to occupy their time. One of their favorites had been an ongoing discussion of the greatest action movie ever made. They would be the ones to make it, just as soon as one of them hit the lottery or became independently wealthy. The movie would star actors both living and dead—Bruce Willis, John Wayne, Jason Statham, Steve McQueen, Clint Eastwood, Al Pacino, Robert De Niro, Christopher Walken, Keith David, Harvey Keitel, Lee Van Cleef, Mickey Rourke, Samuel L. Jackson,

Bruce Lee, Jet Li, Fred Williamson, Rowdy Roddy Piper, Jack Nicholson, Lee Marvin, Kurt Russell, Mel Gibson, Sylvester Stallone, Arnold Schwarzenegger, Jean-Claude Van Damme, Steve Buscemi, Michael Madsen, Tom Sizemore, Jackie Chan, Rutger Hauer, Thomas Jane, Christian Bale, Christopher Lambert, Charles Bronson, Ice-T, The Rock, Lee Majors, Ken Foree, William Shatner, Sean Connery, and Chuck Norris. The plot, such as it was, involved putting all of the actors together on the set and letting them shoot guns at each other for two and a half hours. There would be lots of explosions. And the title—the title was perfect.

Fuck Around Quotient Zero.

"We could use some of that right about now," Jeff said.

"Yeah," Scott agreed. "That's what I was thinking, too. I god-damned guarantee you that Jason Statham would have been out of this cage by now."

"Well," Roy said softly, "you're not Jason Statham and I'm damn sure not Clint Eastwood."

"You're old enough to be," Scott teased.

"Fuck you."

"I still think Hollywood ripped us off," Jeff said. "The Expendables? That shit was our idea."

The four of them sat down in a circle and waited. The air ducts banged and thrummed each time the ventilation kicked on. Occasionally, one of them would stretch or lean against the wire mesh, rattling it. But otherwise, the warehouse was silent. They sat like that for a long time before they became aware of a new sound—a different sound; one that they weren't used to hearing. It was barely audible—so slight, in fact, that at first Jeff wondered privately if he was just hearing things. He was the first to call it to the others' attention.

The noise was coming from the store—an electronic hiss. Not quite static, but close. It lacked the rhythmic, staccato roar of static, and there was a high-pitched whine beneath it, barely noticeable.

"What is it?" Scott whispered.

Roy shrugged. "The emergency broadcast system,

maybe?"

Jeff tilted his head and listened. "No. I can hardly hear it, but it's not that. This is something different."

Jared stirred beside him, then slowly got to his feet and walked to the door of the cage. He stared out into the warehouse.

"It sounds like outer space," he said after a moment.

Scott stood up. "What are you talking about?"

Jared turned to face them. "NASA has this thing on their website where you can listen to audio from one of their deep space probes. It sounds just like that."

"Sounds more like tinnitus to me," Roy said. "That's what I thought it was, at first. I get ringing in my ears sometimes."

"You never told us that," Scott said.

"That's because I didn't want you guys making fun of me. Clint and I get enough old men jokes around here."

"Could it be tinnitus?" Scott asked.

"Not unless you guys are suffering from it, too. You hear it too, right?"

"He's turned on the televisions," Jeff said, joining Jared alongside the chain link mesh. "That's all it is. A signal of some kind."

"I'm telling you," Jared insisted, "it's outer space. That's the same sound the stars and the sun make."

"Stars and suns are the same thing," Jeff said. "And that's stupid, Jared. How could he possibly have located a signal from outer space?"

"Maybe he's on the NASA website. Maybe he got Carlos or Clint to patch it through one of the home theatre stations or the audio board."

"Too bad he couldn't patch through some Wu Tang Clan instead," Scott joked.

Jeff noticed that Roy had an intense look of concentration on his face. The older man's head was tilted slightly to one side. He frowned, listening. The lines and creases around his eyes and mouth and nose seemed to deepen.

"What's up, Roy? What are you thinking?"

"I'm thinking that I know what it is," Roy said softly. "And the reason I know what it is, is because I'm an old man. You kids wouldn't know anything about this."

Scott joined them at the side of the cage. "So what is it then?"

"Any of you ever listen to anything on vinyl?"

Jeff, Jared, and Scott all shook their heads.

"Jesus Christ. None of your parents had record albums?"

"Mine did," Jeff said. "Billy Idol. Duran Duran. Quiet Riot. A few others that I can't remember. But they didn't have a turntable to play them on."

"Mine had some, too," Jared said. "I think they sold them at a yard sale when I was a kid, though."

"That sound you hear," Roy said, nodding at the closed door leading into the store, "is the sound at the end of a record album. When the needle reaches the end, if the record isn't scratched, and the turntable doesn't have an automatic return feature on the arm, the record just keeps spinning round and round, and the needle stays stuck in the very last groove. That's the sound it makes. Sort of a crackly, quiet sound."

The three of them glanced at the door and then back at Roy.

"So he's playing records?" Scott asked. "That makes about as much sense as Jared's theory."

"I'm not saying that it's supposed to make sense," Roy countered. "Nothing the man has done tonight makes sense. Shooting people until you get down to six survivors doesn't make sense. Locking everyone in a cage doesn't make sense. But that's what he did. And I'm telling you, that noise we're hearing is the sound at the end of a record."

"If that's so," Jeff whispered, "then what the hell does it mean?"

Shrugging, Roy sat down with his back against the mesh. *That* I couldn't tell you. It means he's crazy, I guess. But we knew that already."

Jeff slid down next to him. Scott began to pace again. Jared remained standing, still listening to the strange noise.

He didn't sit down again until the ventilation system came back on, drowning out the sound. Jared's stomach growled, loud enough that Jeff could hear it over the rumbling air ducts.

"Sorry," he apologized. The tips of his ears turned red. "I'm hungry."

"Don't apologize," Jeff told him. "I'm fucking starved. I'd kill for some pizza from Jim and Nena's right about now."

"I'm surprised you didn't say Olive Garden," Scott said. "Doesn't what's her face still work there?"

"Michelle?" Jeff shrugged. "Yeah, I think so. I haven't talked to her in months, though."

"That's a shame," Roy said. "I liked her."

Scott nodded. "Me, too. I miss her."

Jeff rolled his eyes and groaned. "The only thing you guys miss is the free take-out she used to bring us when we were dating."

"True," Roy laughed. "But it's not every day that one of your co-workers is dating the manager of an Olive Garden. Opportunities like that—and food like that—don't come along too often in life."

"Seriously, though," Scott said. "Why did you guys break up? You never did tell us."

Jeff shifted uncomfortably. "I don't know. She was really nice. Beautiful. Great in bed. But I just didn't feel about her the way I did about April."

Scott and Roy nodded. Jared said nothing.

"You talk to April lately?" Scott asked.

"No. But you better believe the first thing I'm going to do when we get out of here is give her a call."

"That's a good idea," Roy said. "You guys won't understand until you're my age, but it all goes so fast."

"What does?" asked Jeff.

"Life. One day you're twenty-five and you've got life by the balls. The next, you wake up and your balls are hanging down by your knees and your bones creak and your hair is gone—or gray. Your kids don't know you, your wife barely tolerates you. You're a stranger in your own house. And a stranger in the mirror, too. And when that happens, you look back on the last few decades and wonder where they went."

None of them responded. In truth, they weren't sure what to say.

"Call her," Roy whispered, his voice thick with urgency and emotion. "If you love her, when we get out of here, call her and let her know, Jeff. Life is too short to dick around. Trust me on this."

Jeff nodded thoughtfully. "I will."

"At least you all have somebody," Jared muttered. "I mean, even if you aren't together, at least you've got memories to look back on and stuff."

"Surely you have an ex?" Roy asked.

Jared shook his head. "No. There's nobody. There never has been. I've always wanted—"

The door swung open, slamming into the wall behind it and booming across the warehouse. The strange sound grew louder, but still, none of them could identify it. The killer strode in. His shoes tapped loudly on the concrete as he quickly approached the cage. Once again, Jeff noticed that he was still armed only with the pistol. The machete and the shotgun were missing. Jeff noticed something else as the gunman inserted the key into the lock. There was blood on his knuckles and in the webbing between his fingers. It glistened in the fluorescent lights.

Scott whispered. His voice was so low that Jeff had to strain to hear him.

"Fuck around quotient zero."

Jeff tensed. His hands curled into fists.

The intruder slipped the lock off and opened the door. His other hand clutched the pistol, which he leveled at them. His expression was stoic. He glanced at each of them, and then his gaze finally settled on Jared.

"You. What's your name?"

"J-Jared." His voice was so soft that Jeff had trouble hearing him.

"Okay, Jared. It's your turn. I need you to come with me."
Jared took three steps backward. "My turn? What do you
mean? What are you doing out there? Where are Carlos and
Clint?"

"They're in the store. I'll show you."

Jared skittered further backward. "I'm not going
anywhere with you."

"Okay." The man raised the pistol and pointed it at
Jared's head. "Suit yourself."

His finger flexed on the trigger in an almost loving
caress. Jared flung his hands up over his face and shrieked.
The intruder strode into the cage and reached for him. At the
same time, Scott lunged forward, grabbing for the gun.

"Motherfucker," Scott shouted. "We've had it with your
shit!"

The man in black side-stepped the attack, lowered
the pistol, and squeezed the trigger. The explosion was
deafening. Smoke filled the cage. Jeff and Roy darted to the
rear wall as Scott collapsed, screaming. The killer seized
Scott's hair in his fist and yanked hard. Scott wailed louder.
Jeff turned around long enough to see blood jetting from a
hole in Scott's pants. He'd been shot in the knee.

Without a word, the gunman dragged Scott through the
door and out of the cage. Yelling at the others to help him,
Scott grasped at the concrete floor. Jeff leaped forward,
shouting his name, but halted as the killer raised the pistol
and pointed it at him. Roy stood at Jeff's side, visibly
shaking. Jared had collapsed in the corner, his face hidden
in his hands. His sobs were almost as loud as Scott's shrieks.

"Scott…" Jeff's voice was hoarse.

"Stay there," the man in black said. He slammed Scott's
head onto the floor and placed one black-booted foot on
Scott's shoulder blades. Then he swung the door shut and
locked the cage again. Scott groaned. Blood leaked from the
gunshot in his knee and pooled on the floor. The intruder
grabbed Scott's hair again and jerked his head up. Then,
keeping the gun trained on the injured man, he let go of his

hair and seized his foot instead. Grunting, he began to drag Scott across the warehouse. Screaming and fighting, Scott scrabbled for a grip on the concrete. His fingernails caught in a crack, and he held on. Spit frothed on his lips. His eyes rolled.

"No," he cried. "No, no, no, no, no…Amanda! *AMANDA!"*

The intruder tugged harder, and Scott's fingernails peeled away like the skin of a grape. He wailed as he was dragged across the warehouse. His bleeding fingers and knee left red trails in their wake.

"Scott," Jeff hollered. "Bring him back, you fuck! Leave him alone. Scott? Fight him, Scott. Don't let him take you!"

Scott responded to his friend's cries with another shriek. Then the man in black dragged him through the door and it slammed shut behind them, muffling his screams. They heard a great commotion from the other side of the door. Then Scott was silenced in mid-cry. In the aftermath of the sudden violence, his silence somehow seemed much worse.

"Jesus," Roy panted. His face was ashen and covered in sweat. Clutching his chest, he slid down the wall and sank to the floor. "Oh my sweet Jesus."

Jared wept—great, wracking sobs that seemed to explode from his chest.

Jeff wrapped his fingers around the chain links, shook the wire mesh, and shouted until his throat was raw and his voice was hoarse.

And beneath it all, the strange noise continued, and when it grew louder, they barely noticed.

FOUR

"We're fucked," Jeff moaned. "We are absolutely one hundred and ten percent fucked. Do not pass go. Do not collect two hundred dollars. There's no 'Get Out Of Jail Free' card. We're just...*fucked*."

"Stop saying that," Jared wailed. "Just stop it! I don't want to hear it anymore. You're just making things worse."

"Well that's too damned bad, Jared. If you want to hold hands and sing Kumba-fucking-ya, then be my guest. But leave me the hell out of it."

Five, maybe ten minutes had passed since Scott's abduction. Jeff had no way of knowing for sure, but it didn't seem like any longer than that. Scott's bloodstains were still fresh—not yet dried and brown.

"Both of you knock it off," Roy wheezed. He sat with his back against the wall, his collar unbuttoned and his tie hanging loose. His sleeves were rolled up and his shirttail hung out loosely over his hips. Roy's expression had gone from pale to alabaster, and the sweat on his face had increased to the point where his skin shone like he was lathered in cooking oil. Big droplets of perspiration rolled down his cheeks and the back of his neck. His breathing came in short gasps, and he kept flexing the fingers on his left hand.

"Are you okay?" Jared asked him. A thin layer of snot coated Jared's upper lip. Jared didn't seem to notice.

"No, I'm most definitely not okay. Do I look okay to you?"

"No. That's why I asked."

"I'm having chest pains. And you've got snot on your lip."

Jared wiped his lip with his shirt sleeve.

"Is it a heart attack?" Jeff asked.

Roy shrugged. "Maybe. Maybe not. It could be angina. It could just be gas or stress, or maybe a pulled muscle. Or it could be the big one. All I know is that it hurts like a son of a bitch and I can't breathe. It feels like somebody is squeezing my chest. And I'm tired. God, I'm tired."

"Just lie back," Jared said. "Try to take it easy until help arrives."

Jeff snorted. "Oh, come on, man. Are you high? Help isn't arriving. I'm telling you, we're fucked."

"Shut up!" Jared whirled around to face him. "I mean it, Jeff, if you say that one more time, I'll—"

"You'll what, Jared? Beat me up? Kill me? Well go ahead, dude. Come on. Give it your best shot. If I'm lucky, maybe you'll kill me before he does."

Roy tried to speak but broke into a violent fit of coughing, and Jared and Jeff fell silent, glancing at him in concern.

"Jeff," Roy rasped. "Stop it. You've been our rock through all of this. If it weren't for you, the rest of us would have freaked out already."

"We're already freaked out," Jeff said.

"Even worse than we've already done. You're the one that's been holding things together. You're the glue. We need you to stay strong. *I* need you to stay strong. I'm scared and I'm worried and I'm in a lot of pain right now. I need somebody to lean on. So be that person, okay? Please?"

"I'm sorry," Jeff said. His voice softened, but simultaneously took on a higher pitch. He kneeled next to the older salesman. "I'll try. It's just…Scott. I can't get the image out of my head, you know? Every time I try, I hear the gunshot. Hear him screaming. His fingernails are still lying out there on the floor. His blood is still there, too, and it's still wet and all I keep thinking is who will clean it up?"

Neither man answered him. Jared closed his eyes, turned away and sighed. Roy just stared at Jeff and continued flexing his fingers and shaking his hand. Tears streamed down Jeff's cheeks. His Adam's apple bobbed up and down. He took a deep breath and shuddered.

"Who's gonna clean it up?" he asked again. "Who's gonna get us out of here? His fingernails came off and they're still out there on the floor and that fucker shot him—that fucker shot Scott in the goddamned knee and all he wanted to do was pick up his girlfriend and take her out for her birthday."

"I know," Roy whispered. "I know. But there's nothing we can do about it now."

"But there has to be," Jeff insisted. "There has to be something we can do. I mean, otherwise, what's the point? What's the fucking point of it all? Why did I go through high school and college, put up with all kinds of bullshit in life, watch my grandfather die of cancer, go through that break up with April, and stick with this stupid job? Why go through all of that if I was just going to end up inside this cage? It doesn't make any sense."

"No," Roy agreed. "It doesn't."

"Did you guys hear Scott when that crazy fuck dragged him out of here? Scott always seemed so strong, you know? But not at the end. I'm not going out like that. Not after everything that's happened tonight. I mean, what's the fucking point? Bill and Alan are dead. Clint and Carlos are missing. Scott's been shot. For all we know, maybe they're dead, too. But we're still alive, right?"

Roy nodded. "Yes, we are. That's my point."

"Well, that means something. We must be alive for a reason. I can't die in this cage, man. That just doesn't make any sense. I want to live, Roy. I want to live."

"Then hold on to that. Own it. Let it drive you and direct you."

"I'm scared, Roy."

"I'm scared, too. We all are. I've never been more scared in my life. But you need to get it together. Now promise me."

"Okay." Nodding, Jeff wiped his nose with his hand. "I promise."

"Listen," Jared interrupted. He held up his hand to silence them.

"What?" Jeff glanced around. "What is it?"

Jared stood up and walked over to the door of the cage. Then he turned around and faced them.

"You guys don't hear that?"

Roy frowned. "Hear what?"

"The noise. The one that sounds like space? It's changed."

Jeff and Roy both fell silent and listened. After a moment, Jeff stirred.

"He's right. It has changed."

"I can't hear much of anything," Roy said. "My ears are still ringing. What does it sound like now?"

"There are chimes," Jared whispered. "My mother has wind chimes hanging on her deck. It sort of sounds like those, except that it's just the same four notes over and over again."

Jeff nodded. "I hear them, too—just beneath the static sound. But they're getting louder."

"I was wrong, after all," Jared said. "Scott was right. It doesn't sound like space. It doesn't sound like anything. It just sounds… *wrong*."

"Ignore it," Roy wheezed.

"I can't." Jared tapped his head with his index finger. "It's inside my head, like cold razors going across my brain. You don't feel that?"

"I told you—my ears are ringing. I can't hear shit. Between the last gunshot, the stress, and my tinnitus, I'm lucky I can still hear you guys at all."

Jeff rubbed his arms and shivered. His legs had gone to sleep while he'd crouched on the floor. He stomped his feet to get the circulation back into them. Gooseflesh prickled his forearms.

"Is it me," he asked, "or is it getting colder in here?"

"I've been cold since my chest started hurting," Roy replied, "but I'm sweating like a pig."

"It's cold," Jared agreed. "It happened around the same time the noise changed."

"Maybe he opened the outside doors or something," Jeff suggested. "Maybe we were right, earlier. Maybe he's looting the store, and he's got a van or a box truck or something pulled up out front."

"That doesn't explain the wind chimes," Jared said.

"Fuck the wind chimes!"

"Jeff." Roy's tone was cautionary. "Come on. You promised me you'd keep it together."

The warehouse door banged open again, and the odd noise filled the cage. The chiming sound had a rhythm unlike any that Jeff had ever heard. Combined with the static, it seemed to pulse and throb, ebb and flow. It washed over them, hypnotic, yet unsettling. Jeff was so captivated by it that he forgot all about the man in black until he heard his footsteps on the concrete. As he drew closer, Jeff noticed that the madman's lower lip was bloodied and swollen.

He punched him, Jeff thought. *Scott—or one of the other guys—got in a swing at him!*

"Things are moving now," the killer reported, the hint of a smile on his formerly expressionless face. "I'm already set for the next one."

"Leave us alone," Jeff grumbled. "Why can't you just leave us the fuck alone?"

"And what is your name?"

"Fuck you. I'm not telling you my name. How's that?"

The killer shrugged. "That's okay. I don't need your name. It's just nice to have. Names have power, but at this point, we can forego them. How about I call you Next instead? Because that is what you are. You're next."

The blood drained from Jeff's face.

"No." Roy reached out with one hand and steadied himself against the wall. Then he slowly got to his feet, gritting his teeth and grunting with exertion. "Whatever it is you're doing out there, take me next."

The man in black blinked.

"Roy…" Jeff pawed at the older man's sleeve, but Roy shrugged him away.

"No, Jeff. Leave it alone." He turned to the intruder. "How about it? Why not let these guys stay back here a while longer? They're scared. Take me instead."

The lunatic's smile grew wider. "You're not scared?"

"Of course I'm scared. But I'm also tired, and to tell the

truth, I'm not feeling so hot right now."

"What's wrong with you?"

"I'm old."

"Okay." The madman unlocked the cage. "Makes no difference to me. You can go next. Come on."

"Roy!" Jeff reached for him again. "What the hell are you thinking? Don't do this."

"He's right," Jared whispered. "Don't go out there. You don't know what's going to happen."

Roy gently removed Jeff's hand from his shoulder and stepped away from him. Then he looked at them both and smiled.

"It will be okay, guys. You'll see. Just stay here."

Jeff shook his head. "No way. No fucking way. You—"

"Let's go," the intruder shouted. "You volunteered. No take backs. Time is short. The signal is getting stronger."

"You heard the man," Roy said. "We don't want to interrupt his signal. It all sounds very important."

He winked at Jeff and Jared and then limped out of the cage before they could stop him.

The man in black closed the door and locked it again. The padlock thumped against the steel mesh. Then he motioned Roy forward.

"What's your name?"

"My name is Roy. Roy Hembeck. And you are?"

The gunman paused in mid-step, clearly taken aback.

"My name is Simon," he answered after a long pause.

"Simon what?"

"That's all you get. Names are power."

"So you've said."

Simon raised the pistol and pointed it at Roy's midsection. "Walk."

Jeff called after Roy as they strolled across the warehouse, but the older salesman never looked back. He coughed once, and his knees buckled. For a moment, Jeff thought he might collapse in the middle of the aisle. But then Roy seemed to regain his strength, and marched slowly toward the door with his head held high. Simon followed closely behind him, clutching the pistol firmly. Then the door closed behind them, and the sound of the signal—whatever it was—became muffled again.

Jared sat down and cradled his face in his hands.

Jeff glanced at the floor and noticed that one of them— Simon or Roy—had stepped in a pool of Scott's blood. Scarlet footprints led all the way to the closed door. Then they disappeared.

"And soon," he said out loud, "so will we. Just like the others. We'll disappear."

If Jared heard him, he didn't respond.

Jeff stared at the footprints and waited to see which one of them would be next.

FIVE

"Maybe Roy had a plan," Jeff said. "Maybe he was going to try something. Maybe he'd figured out a way to escape and he didn't want to tell us because he was worried we might let it slip."

Jeff and Jared were seated in the middle of the cage again. The temperature had grown even colder, so they'd used old video game system boxes to sit on, rather than sitting on the chilly concrete floor.

"Maybe he was faking the chest pains," Jeff continued. "Make Simon think he was weak—not a threat. And then he was going to rush him or something. Run out the door. Simon locked the door behind him after he shot Alan, but if Roy was quick, I bet he could smash through the glass. And did you notice? Simon had a fat fucking lip. Scott or somebody punched him in the mouth. So he's not infallible."

Jared didn't respond.

"Or maybe," Jeff continued, "he was going to do something with that book of matches. Maybe he was going to light the fucking store on fire. Get the firemen and police here."

"Jeff?"

"Yeah?"

"What do you think happens to us when we die?"

Jared sounded tired. Jeff knew how he felt. He was exhausted, too. Maybe the adrenalin was leaving his system, or maybe it was some kind of delayed shock. Whatever the reason, Jeff wanted nothing more at that moment than to lie down on the floor, close his eyes, and go to sleep. He would dream of April and his parents and friends he'd known in high school and college, and in the dream, they would all be happy and smiling, and he and his friends would have never grown up and had to get jobs and he wouldn't be here. He'd be somewhere safe and warm.

"Do you think there's a Heaven?" Jared asked. "A God?

And if so, do you have to go through all that born again stuff, or is it okay if you just tried to live a good life?"

"I don't know," Jeff yawned. "My parents took me to Golgotha Lutheran Church every week when I was a little kid, but I never really paid attention. We quit going there after a while."

"How come you stopped going?"

"There was some kind of scandal. I don't remember what, exactly. I was just a little kid. The caretaker raped some girls in the cemetery or something like that. Whatever it was, my parents seemed to lose interest in God after that."

"I never went," Jared said. "I thought about it sometimes. My Grandma was Catholic, but my parents never let her take me to church."

"Why not?"

"They were atheists. My Dad said that he didn't want me getting indoctrinated."

"I think you have to be born again. You've got to ask Jesus to come into your heart or something, and forgive you for your sins."

"That's all?"

Jeff shrugged. "I think so. Like I said, it's been a long time."

They fell quiet for a while. Jeff blinked. His eyelids felt heavy. The air ducts rattled. The air grew colder. The strange noise from out in the store grew louder. Occasionally, he felt it throb in his chest, like the bass notes from a subwoofer did if you turned the volume up high. Jeff yawned again, not bothering to cover his mouth with his hand. Jared glanced up at him.

"How can you be sleepy?"

"I'm usually in bed by now."

"On a Wednesday night?"

"Sure. Why?"

"I don't know," Jared said. "I figured you'd be going out on dates or something. I was always jealous of you and Scott and Ray and Clint. You guys seemed to have exciting lives."

61

"Not on a work night. Not for me, at least. I just go home and crash. There's nothing good on television on Wednesday nights."

"Sure there is. I watch *Castaways*."

"*Castaways* jumped the shark a long time ago, dude. And besides, it's off by the time I get home. You know what sucks? Working in this place and selling TiVo and DVR shit all day, and then not having them when I go home."

Jared nodded. They both fell silent for a few minutes.

"Jeff?"

"What?"

"I'm sorry about earlier. For the way I acted and what I said."

"It's okay, Jared. I'm sorry, too. I was being a real dick."

"No you weren't. You were just frightened. We both were."

"Well, it still didn't give me the right to holler at you. So I apologize."

"Apology accepted." Jared grinned. "But you're wrong about *Castaways*. Best show on television."

Jeff snickered quietly, then chuckled, and then threw back his head and laughed. Jared joined him, slapping his thigh. The two of them sat there giggling until their eyes watered.

"Shit," Jeff sighed. "That felt good. I needed that."

"Yeah." Jared nodded.

"So…"

"So."

Jared's expression grew serious again. "What are we going to do when he comes back?"

"I don't know. We could try rushing him and tag-team his ass."

"I can't. I'm sorry, but I just can't. Especially after watching him shoot Scott in the knee like that."

"Well, don't feel too bad. To be honest, I don't think we'd get away with it anyway."

"So what do we do?"

"You mean which one of us goes next?"

Jared nodded.

"We could draw straws," Jeff suggested.

"But we don't have any straws."

"Well, then I guess the only thing we can do is wait."

"That's it?"

"That's it. Unless you can think of something?"

"Maybe do what you said. We could try to attack him when he opens the cage the next time."

"No. You were right. Not after what happened to Scott."

"I thought what Scott did was very brave."

"But it didn't work out for him, did it?"

Jared didn't respond. Jeff stifled another yawn. Then he scooted his box over to the wall, leaned backward, crossed his arms, and closed his eyes. He let his chin droop down to touch his chest and focused on his breathing so that he wouldn't have to think about anything else.

Jared mumbled a whispered prayer. "Dear Jesus, please forgive me for my sins. I accept you into my heart. Please don't let me die in here."

He paused. At first, Jeff thought he was finished.

"Is that how it's done, Jeff?"

"I guess so. Sounded okay to me."

"Thank you, Jesus," Jared said. "I'm so sorry. Please…"

Jeff tuned him out, but he couldn't tune out the signal, humming insistently in the background.

When Jeff woke up again, Jared was screaming.

Jeff didn't move. Not a muscle. Not a twitch. He kept his eyes squeezed shut, made sure his breathing seemed regular, and pretended to be asleep. He didn't need to see to know what was happening. He could hear it.

"No," Jared squealed. "I don't want to go. Jeff, wake up! I'm not going to go out there. You can't make me."

"Stop it."

"Leave me alone! Get away from me ri—"

Flesh smacked against flesh. Jeff was pretty sure that

Simon had just slapped Jared across the face. He resisted the urge to jump at the sound. Jared continued to sob and shriek. Another smack rang out, followed by a more solid, meaty thud. Jared fell silent, as if someone had flipped a switch. Jeff wondered what had happened, but he kept his eyes shut. Perhaps Simon had pistol-whipped Jared, or maybe he'd knocked him out cold. He heard Simon grunt, heard the chain links jingle, and then Jared began to scream again.

"Take Jeff instead! Not me. Take him. He wanted to rush you. He's the one who's disobeyed."

Bitch, Jeff thought. *I see how you are.*

"Take him," Jared insisted. "Get him instead of me! He was plotting against you the whole time."

"He'll get his turn."

"Oh Jesus. Oh Jesus, help me! I don't want to die."

"Want me to shoot you in the balls?"

"No, no, no, no, n—"

"Then quit wiggling."

"Please. Please, please, please! Jeff, wake up! I don't want to die."

"Stop it!"

"I don't want to die. I don't want to—"

He was interrupted by a third smack. Jared groaned, and then went quiet for a moment. Simon's boots echoed off the concrete. Then Jared began to yell—a high-pitched, keening wail that seemed to have no end. It went on and on and on, drowning out Simon's threats and the ever-present sound of the signal. Jeff had to focus to hear the sound of the padlock snapping shut. Jared's cries lasted until Simon had dragged him out of the warehouse. The door swung shut again. Silence returned to the cage.

Jeff kept his eyes closed. He felt safer in the dark than he did in the harsh, yellow glow of the fluorescent lighting. In the dark, you couldn't see the monsters when they came to get you.

SIX

The signal swelled, booming throughout the warehouse. The fluorescent light fixtures swung back and forth, creaking on their chains and raining dust down onto cardboard boxes full of various home electronics, which were also swaying. The fire extinguisher fell from its hook on the wall and crashed onto the floor, then rolled out of sight. The wire mesh of the cage trembled and clanged.

Jeff opened his eyes, unsure of what was happening or how long he'd been sleeping. Yawning, he stood up and stretched, wondering for a brief second where he was, and what the hell he was hearing. Then he remembered, and the realization was like a kick in the gut. The noise made his teeth and ears ache. His feet were numb—asleep. He stumbled around, wondering why the signal had gotten louder. And then he saw why.

The warehouse door stood open again.

And Simon walked toward him.

It was his turn.

"Shit."

He mouthed the word, but realized that he couldn't hear his own voice over the roar. The sound throbbed up through the floor, boring through his feet and then his legs and then surging into the rest of him. Jeff felt it rumbling in his chest. His ears and nose felt blocked, like he was in an airplane making its ascent or descent. He wished they would pop. More dust drifted down from the ceiling, making his nose and throat itch. Jeff's eyes watered.

Simon didn't speak. He didn't have to. The big, black pistol in his hand said everything. Jeff knew the drill. He'd seen it happen enough this evening. Simon would unlock the cage. Jeff would step out. The two of them would walk across the warehouse and disappear through the door.

He would not come back. Of this Jeff was certain. He didn't know what was happening on the other side of the door. He didn't know what Simon was up to. He didn't know if his friends and co-workers were alive or dead, but he knew that once they'd taken this walk with their captor, none of them had returned. And neither would he.

"Please?"

It was all Jeff could say. He hoped it would be enough.

It wasn't. Simon pulled out Alan's key ring for the last time, unlocked the cage, and opened the door. If he'd heard Jeff's singular plea over the cacophony of white noise, he gave no indication. He simply stood back, pointed the gun at Jeff, and waited. Jeff noticed that the gunman was no longer wearing his sunglasses. When Jeff didn't move, Simon gestured again, impatient. The signal grew even louder.

Jeff took a deep breath, held it, and then stepped forward. His legs felt wobbly. His feet tingled. He had to reach out and grab the chain links to keep from falling. Simon watched this impassively. Jeff stared into his captor's eyes—those two dark circles, devoid of any emotion, and Simon stared back without blinking. Then, Jeff found himself at the door. He exhaled as he left the cage.

Simon motioned with the gun, not bothering to lock the cage behind him. Jeff shuffled forward and Simon fell in step behind him. The killer placed the barrel of the pistol against the small of Jeff's back. Jeff felt the cold steel through the material of his dress shirt, grating against his spine. Simon leaned close to Jeff's ear. His sour breath smelled of cheese.

"Your name is Jeff?"

Jeff nodded, unable to speak.

"You are six. The most important number of all. Some say that seven and thirteen are the power numbers, but for what we do tonight, it is six. You should feel very proud."

Jeff nodded again, feigning understanding and hoping to placate the madman.

Simon prodded him with the gun. "Let's go. You know the way."

Yes, Jeff thought. *I sure do. How many times have I walked through this warehouse and out into the store? A thousand? A million? Every time I go to the bathroom or take a lunch break or make a sale and come back here to get the item for the customer, I go through that door.*

He'd never paused to consider it. Never thought about such a trivial act. But now, faced with the knowledge that this could very well be his last time doing so, it was all that Jeff *could* think about. His feet were no longer asleep, but now they felt heavy—weighted with sixty-pound bags of cement. He stopped, but Simon pushed harder with the gun. Jeff began walking again, past rows of televisions and stereos and speakers and microwaves. The door loomed before him. The sign overtop of it read "EXIT" in bright red block letters.

But this is not an exit, he thought. *This is an entrance. An entrance into the store.*

Exit. Entrance. Maybe it's the same thing, depending on your perspective.

Jesus fucking Christ, I'm really going to die, aren't I?

April…I'm so sorry, hon. I should have contacted you. I should have said what I've wanted to say. I love you. I never stopped loving you…

He halted again, and when Simon urged him forward, Jeff resisted by spreading his feet and locking his knees.

"Move."

"I want to know something first." Jeff had to shout above the noise.

"Speak. But you try anything, and I'll put a bullet through both of your kneecaps."

"What happens when we go through the door?"

Simon was silent. For a moment, Jeff thought that maybe the madman had answered his question and he just hadn't heard it. But then Simon spoke.

"We're opening the door."

"I know that. I watched you take the others through it. I'm asking you what happens after we go through the door."

"You misunderstand me. I said that we're opening a door. I wasn't talking about this door. Now move."

"Blow me."

Simon frowned.

Jeff grinned. "What happened to your lip? Was it Scott? Did he deck your ass? And where's your sunglasses? You got punched, didn't you motherfucker?"

Glowering, Simon shoved Jeff hard.

Jeff stumbled forward, nearly falling. "Hey! Motherfucker..."

"I said move! Open that door or I'll open your belly. Your choice. Makes no difference to me."

Jeff made the remaining twelve paces to the exit, his brief surge of anger and bravado overcome once more by fear. Simon followed along closely behind him. The strange signal grew louder with each step. Jeff noticed that its tone had changed again. The chimes were still there, but they were mere background noise now. The dominant sound was a deep, rumbling hum—constant and unbroken, accompanied by wave after wave of crackling static, buzzing like a swarm of monstrous, angry bees. He felt it rumble in his chest.

"What is that?" he shouted. "Where's it coming from?"

Although he wasn't turned around to face Simon, Jeff could tell that the intruder was grinning. He could hear it in Simon's voice.

"It's Shtar. Open the door and I'll show you."

Jeff stretched his arm towards the door. It seemed to take forever. He placed his palm against the cool wood, and felt the vibrations running through it.

"Fuck around quotient zero..."

With a final, futile sigh of resignation, he pushed the door open and stepped through. The sound hit him with its full fury. Jeff felt as if he'd been struck. Disoriented, he paused again, but Simon shoved him forward. Jeff glanced around the store in shock, trying to process what he was seeing.

Every television and audio component in the store had been turned on. The signal blasted from a hundred different sources and speakers. All of the television screens showed the same image—a constantly-shifting sea of black and white speckled static. Inside the static, deep within the center of the screens, something moved—a roiling, writhing tubular mass, also composed of static but distinguishable from the specks around it in the manner of a 3D image. It was difficult for Jeff to make out its shape, but it reminded him of a sun with tentacles sprouting from it. Orbs of white light revolved around the shape and darted across the screens, dancing amidst the snow.

"Isn't it beautiful?" Simon sounded absolutely ecstatic, even as he shouted above the roar.

Jeff tried to respond, but found that he couldn't. His breath caught in his throat. His lungs ached. His pulse began to throb in his temples, keeping time with the steady, monotonous throb pouring from everywhere around him. All that he could do was slowly shake his head back and forth. His gaze darted around the store. Bill and Alan's bodies still lay where they'd fallen. The front door was still closed and presumably locked. The parking lot was still empty.

"Rejoice," Simon hollered. "He is coming! This is his hour and I have opened the doorway. Shtar is coming through."

"I don't know what you're talking about!"

"You sell this stuff," Simon yelled, guiding Jeff across the store. They had to step over Alan's corpse. "You know all about the switch to digital television. I'm sure you sold plenty of converter boxes and answered plenty of customer's questions."

In truth, Jeff hadn't. The majority of residents in York County, Pennsylvania, were either on cable or satellite television hook-ups. The only people impacted by the digital conversion had been those living in the rural parts of the county who still used television antennas, and those folks were more likely to shop at Wal-Mart than they were a high-end store like Big Bill's Home Electronics.

"Didn't you ever wonder," Simon continued, "what would happen to all of those old broadcast channels once they stopped transmitting? Didn't you ever think about it?

Yes, the government told us that some of the frequencies were being used by emergency services, but how many channels do your local fire department need? What about all those empty channels? The obsolete ones?"

Jeff turned to face him, no longer caring if Simon shot him or not. At least in death, he'd be able to escape the sound.

"That is Shtar's domain," Simon continued. "That was where he lurked. He waited inside the empty signals, yearning to be freed. All he needed was someone to open the door for him. That's what we're doing tonight. We're opening a door. Once it is open, he will spread."

"But why us?"

"I needed six. Six to prepare the opening. You and your friends have taken part in a great work. You should be proud."

Blinking, Jeff licked his lips. His mouth was dry, and he tried to work up enough spit to speak. The pressure in his ears and nose increased, making it hard to focus on anything, let alone a clever response.

"You're fucking crazy. You know that, right? You're a god-damned fucking loon."

Simon cocked his head. His jaw twitched. Jeff noticed his finger tighten around the trigger.

"You're not proud?" The gunman sounded astonished and confused. "I bestowed an honor on you."

"No! No, I'm not fucking proud. Where the hell are my friends?"

Simon shook his head sadly. Jeff had to strain to hear him.

"You should be proud. You should be very proud. All those years of study and preparation. All that time spent scouting this location, making sure it was right. Making sure you and your co-workers were right. But here we are, and the moment is at hand, and you have no appreciation for the work."

Jeff balled his hands into fists. "I asked you where my friends are."

"I'll take you to them."

He gestured with the handgun toward the home theatre

section of the store. That area was a specially designed enclosed room, complete with a big-screen television, top-of-the line home theatre system, several couches and recliners, and even a potted plant. Its aim was to reproduce a living or family room experience within the store, which would further convince customers to make a purchase after they had immersed themselves in it. The room had one large bay window and a single door. The door was closed, and the window had been taped over.

"Who punched you?" Jeff asked again, hollering over the noise. "Was it Scott? Or Clint? I bet it was one of them."

"Ask them yourself."

Jeff opened the door to the home theatre room, walked inside...

...and screamed.

Jared, Roy, Scott, Clint and Carlos were lying on the gray-carpeted floor in front of the big-screen television. Their bodies had been positioned with their heads close together and their feet and legs wide apart, like spokes on a wheel—the television forming the central point in that wheel. They faced upward, their eyes open, their mouths gaping. Each of their throats had been cut. No, Jeff realized. Not cut. They'd been hacked open. The bloody machete sat nearby, propped up against one of the recliners.

"Oh God..."

Jeff turned to flee and Simon shot him. He didn't realize it at first. He could barely hear the gun blast over the continuous, overwhelming signal. Something punched him in the stomach—hard. He bent over, the air rushing from his lungs, and crashed against the arm of the couch. His stomach burned. He glanced down and saw blood.

"No you don't," Simon said. "Not now. You are number six. I told you before. You are the most important number of all. Can't open the door without you. I need six. He is waiting."

Clutching his stomach with both hands, Jeff collapsed to his knees and tried to breathe. It was hard to remember how.

The noise was everywhere—seemingly a part of the very air he needed. His ears grew warm. He realized that they were bleeding. Jeff screamed, but couldn't hear himself over the static roar. He caught a glimpse through the window of the televisions in the store. On each of them, the shadowed figure that he'd noticed before was solidifying now. It looked like a tentacle—then a snake—and then an elongated arm. Each shifting form was composed of that crackling black and white static—a simulacrum of white noise and empty transmissions made flesh. A living, breathing broadcast.

Simon kicked him in the back and Jeff fell to the floor face first. His cheek felt wet and sticky. He realized that he'd landed in someone else's blood, and idly wondered whose it was. Scott's, maybe? Or Clint? Yeah, it was probably Clint's blood. He'd been a big guy, after all. He had a lot of blood in him. As Simon grabbed his arm and dragged him across the floor, Jeff wondered who would tell Clint's kids what had happened to their father. Who would tell Scott's girlfriend and Roy's wife? Who would tell Jeff's parents that he loved them?

Who would tell April?

Jeff stared up at Simon as the madman positioned him. The killer's expression was one of glee. Jeff wondered what he was so happy about. Then Simon walked away. Jeff's gaze turned upward. He looked at the television screen. From his vantage point, the image was upside down, but he could still see what was there. He stared at the television. The television stared back. The signal increased yet again, reaching a painful level. Jeff's eardrums popped. His nose began to bleed. He squeezed his eyes shut, wincing. At least his stomach had stopped hurting. If only someone would turn off the noise.

Simon returned, looming over him. He raised the machete over his head. Jeff focused on the blade as it came down. The last thing he heard, buried deep beneath the static and the roar, was the sound of somebody knocking on the store's front door. The blade flashed. The knock came again.

And then, at last, merciful silence returned.

STORY NOTES

This novella was first published as a signed, limited edition hardcover by Cemetery Dance Publications, and was also included in my now out-of-print collection A Conspiracy of One. *This is the first edition available to the mass public. I hope you enjoyed it.*

For two years in the mid-90s, I worked as a salesman for a national home electronics store. I started there as a salesman was eventually promoted to store manager. The job itself sucked. The hours were long and the salesmen worked for commission only, rather than a salary. But we had a lot of fun, just the same. The memories the characters reminisce about while trapped in the cage are all drawn from those experiences, as is the cage itself.

Those experiences were also drawn upon for my short story "Marriage Causes Cancer In Rats", which originally appeared in my long out-of-print collection Fear of Gravity, *and is reprinted here as a special bonus.*

MARRIAGE CAUSES CANCER IN RATS

"It's terminal, Mr. Newton."

Harold stared across the desk. "I'm sorry?"

"Your cancer. Chemotherapy and surgery would be ineffective at this point. Had we caught it earlier, perhaps... I don't understand, Mr. Newton. You had substantial health insurance. Why didn't you come in earlier, at the first sign?"

"I thought they were cysts," Harold told him. "I used to get them all the time when I was a kid. But they were always benign. Just calcium and fatty tissues, they said. It wasn't until the one showed up on my—well, my penis, that I got scared. Can't you cut them out?"

"Not at this point. The cancer has metastasized."

"I think God is trying to kill me," Harold said.

The doctor gave him a puzzled half-smile.

On his way to the car, Harold's vision blurred. He stopped, took several deep breaths, and closed his eyes, waiting for it to pass. Then he opened his eyes again, slid behind the wheel and put the key in the ignition. His hands were trembling.

For the first time in a week, he thought of Marcy, and of Harry Jr. and little Danielle.

And Cecelia.

He began to sob.

On the way home, he called headquarters in Dayton, and told his Regional Manager that he needed a few weeks off, and that somebody else would need to fill in as Store Manager for him. He confided about the cancer, but not the prognosis. The RM agreed that Will, Harold's Assistant Manager, was the obvious choice.

Then Harold stopped into the store and advised Will that he would be running the show. He explained to his sales staff that they'd have to sell big screen TV's and DVD players by themselves for the next few weeks, and that Will was in charge while he was gone.

He didn't tell them about the cancer, but he could see the pity reflected in their eyes just the same. Harold knew what they were thinking: *Poor guy. He's still taking their deaths pretty hard.*

Harold felt the scream welling up from deep inside, and he left the store before it could escape. In the parking lot, the shakes returned and he realized that his face was wet again. He wondered if he'd been crying in front of his employees, and decided that he didn't care. Fuck them and their pity. It was an accusation, even if they didn't know it. It was an accusation because he knew. He knew what they didn't. He hadn't asked for their pity or consolations. Consolation was like a judgment, and though they didn't know, that didn't stop them from judging him just the same.

They didn't know that he'd killed his family.

Or that he'd killed Cecelia, too.

Beneath his skin, Harold's tumors began to throb.

He stopped off at The Coliseum for a drink, and ended up having several. He slammed his fifth shot of Maker's Mark, tried to concentrate on watching the Ravens get their asses handed to them, and found that he couldn't. Those same looks, those knowing stares of pity, followed him here. He saw it reflected in the eyes of the bartender and of the regulars.

He'd never brought Cecelia here, thank God for that. There was nobody to add two plus two, nobody who could say they saw them together. His only tie to the slim dancer was her signature on the receipt for the thirty-two inch Panasonic and matching DVD player he'd sold her, and that was over a year and a half ago.

"Want another one, Harold?" The bartender nodded at his empty shot glass.

He held up his hand, shaking his head. "No, I'm not feeling so good. Think I'm gonna head home."

"You don't look so good, if you don't mind me saying so."

"It's the flu, probably." Harold pulled out his wallet and placed a pile of bills on the bar. His family stared back at him and he snapped the wallet closed. "One of the guys at work had it, and I think he spread it to the whole damn store."

The bartender leaned toward him, his expression that of a conspirator. "That's not what I mean, Harold."

"Well, what then?"

The big man fumbled for the words. "You look—lost. I dunno. Like you're feeling guilty or something."

Harold jumped.

"It's okay, man," the bartender continued, "I know how it must be, going through this, all by yourself."

"You do?" Harold's voice was a whisper.

"Sure I do, man. I mean, how longs it been? Year and a half? Two years almost? You're lonely and you miss your wife, but you don't want to hook up with anybody again because you'd feel guilty. You'd feel like you were cheating on Marcy. But look man, what happened to your family wasn't your fault. You need to—"

Harold didn't hear the rest. The blood pounding in his ears sounded like an onrushing freight train.

He turned and ran out of the bar.

The tumors hurt the whole way home. Stuck in traffic on Interstate 83, the car next to him blasted rap music with the bass cranked to a thunderous level. Wave after wave of sound crashed over Harold and his tumors throbbed with each beat. He reached into the glove compartment, grabbed the aspirin, and downed two of them, grimacing at the taste. With each beat of his heart, there was a twinge in his chest. It hurt to breathe. Then the pain faded, replaced by the ache in his hand. Groaning, he flexed his fingers.

As the traffic crawled along, he shifted his weight, trying to get comfortable. The pain in his hand and chest had shifted to his back and groin, and each movement was agony.

The rap song in the car next to his was over. Now, a pop princess was mangling Elvis Presley's 'Are You Lonesome Tonight'.

"Is your heart filled with pain? Shall I come back again..."

The traffic started to move, and Harold gripped the wheel. He turned his own stereo on in retaliation, searching for escape.

"I used to love her, but I had to kill her…"

Cursing, Harold stabbed the eject button and flung the CD out the window.

He coughed, tasted blood, and reached for two more aspirin. He considered it for a moment, pondering the dangers of consuming aspirin along with the drinks he'd had at the bar, and then swallowed them anyway. What was the worst thing that could happen? He'd die? He was dying anyway, according to the doctor.

By the time he arrived home, Harold could barely stand. He felt the bile rising, and just made it to the toilet when the aspirin, the whiskey, and something that looked like part of his guts came spewing out. When it was over, he wiped his mouth with the back of his hand. It came away red.

He collapsed onto the bed and curled into a ball. He lay there moaning.

Eventually, he slept.

At first, the dreams were nothing more than memories.

It had all been Thom's fault.

Thom Fox had applied for a salesperson's job that October. Harold was short-handed (Branson had been transferred to another store, and the god-damned Nock kid had quit) and the Christmas season was right around the corner. Christmas was their busiest time—a time when all of the salesmen would be working long hours, and when Harold himself would be working seven days a week, open to close. Fortunately, they would also make a lot of money. The salesmen earned commission off of every item they sold, and Harold's managerial bonus was based on their sales volume. Between Thanksgiving and Christmas, they could easily make seventy-five percent of their yearly commission. After the holidays, things would slow down again until air conditioner season.

Despite the fact that Thom Fox had no previous home electronics experience, and even though he looked disheveled and spoke slower than turtle shit, Harold hired him. He had no choice. He needed cannon fodder—somebody to fill in the gaps while the rest of his staff hustled and bustled and glad-handed and asked "How can I help you folks today" or said "Yes, this is the top of the line." Maybe the kid would get lucky, and sell a few microwaves and car stereos. Except the kid couldn't sell, and to help the store's performance (and his own paycheck) Harold began closing Thom's deals.

That was how he'd met Cecelia Ramirez. She'd had her eye on a TV (a Christmas present to herself, she'd said) but was still hesitant. Thom asked Harold to get involved and close the sale.

She was beautiful—a Cuban immigrant with skin the color of light coffee. She had long, raven-black hair that flowed with her every movement. She was slender, graceful, and Harold learned that she was a dancer at the Foxy Lady downtown. Her low-cut jeans hugged her hips in just the right places, and her belly ring gleamed like a diamond.

Harold talked up the television, demonstrating the twin tuner picture-in-picture technology, the black screen for better picture quality, and the benefits of the universal remote. As he did, he felt himself hardening. He was embarrassed, and tried to turn away, but she brushed up lightly against him, smiling as she did.

"It looks awfully hard to hook up," she purred, and her accent almost sent him over the edge right there in the store. He chuckled nervously and backed away.

Her eyes dropped to his crotch and then rose back to his face. "Do you have someone who can hook it up for me?"

"Normally, our salespeople are glad to come to your home and do the installation. You pay them directly for the service. But I'm the manager, and since you're buying the DVD player too, I guess I could do it this evening—no charge."

It had been that easy. He'd read about it (in those phony

letters to Penthouse) and seen it in the movies, but he'd never expected it to happen to him. Harold was thirty-nine, and middle-age had begun to settle upon him. His six-pack abs were lost beneath a small pot belly, and his thinning hair had just begun to sprout some strands of gray. Despite that, this beautiful creature wanted him.

He'd shown up that night, hooked up the television and DVD player, and then accepted her offer of a drink. Half an hour later, they were undressing each other on her couch. They made love in the bedroom, and when Harold awoke at four in the morning, his heart pounded with apprehension.

When he arrived home, Marcy and the kids were sleeping soundly. He hadn't been missed. They never missed him. Things hadn't been good with Marcy for a long time.

"You have my heart." That's what Harold had told her through their first few years of their marriage, holding her at night when she worried about the bills or having children or affording to buy a home.

You have my heart...

By the time he slept with Cecilia, Marcy no longer held that position, and hadn't for quite some time. In the years before the affair, he'd thought often of leaving her, but then Harold Jr. came along, followed a few years later by Danielle. He'd tried to make it all right—to enjoy what he had. Playing baseball in the backyard with Harry and giving horsy rides to Danielle until his back ached. But thirty came and went, and Harold grew resentful. The three of them were like anchors, weighing him down. Marcy was distant, and their lovemaking was nothing more than a ghost—murdered by valiums and antidepressants. Harry Jr. grew into a sullen pre-teen, a stranger, and Danielle decided that she much preferred her mother's company.

His father had died at sixty, his grandfather at sixty-two. The odds didn't look good for him either. That meant his life was half over. At times, Harold could feel his mortality approaching, as surely as the hands ticking on a clock. Cecelia changed that. That first month with her, he felt alive again. He hadn't felt that way since college. She told him she loved him during the second month, murmured it into his neck as he thrust into her. He'd reciprocated the words in the dark, and meant them. She said she wanted him for herself, and made promises in the dark.

Now the dream shifted, as if on fast-forward.

"Don't sweat it," Tony assured him. "We'll make it look like she took off with the kids. The cops will never suspect a thing, as long as you've got your alibi—and as long as you keep your mouth shut."

"Of course I will." Harold was sweating. "Come on, Tony! How long have you guys known me? I've sold Mr. Marano every piece of equipment he's got in his house. You know I wouldn't do that."

"You got the money?" Vince asked around a mouthful of pasta.

Harold handed it to them, and as the envelope exchanged hands he thought, *There's no turning back now. Good. That's good. I'm doing this for Cecelia.*

"How will you—" he began to ask, and then realized he didn't want to know.

Tony took the envelope from Vince and placed it inside his jacket. "We don't ask you why a four-head VCR is better than a two-head. You don't ask us how we do our job. Keep your mouth shut."

But Harold hadn't kept his mouth shut. When his family vanished, Cecelia had been properly sympathetic at first, but Harold could see the relief and sheer glee beneath the surface. Two months later, after an especially frenetic bout of lovemaking, he had told her the truth.

Her reaction was not what he expected, but watching it now through the lens of a dream, Harold didn't know what he had expected. Certainly not for her to slap him, or to reach for the phone, threatening to call the police, which was what she had done.

It replayed in his mind—the struggle, his hands around her throat, her nightgown open beneath him, and as she thrashed, he was both horrified and excited to find that he was aroused again.

After, he'd called Tony, frantic and almost speechless from exertion and shock.

"Don't sweat it," Tony had told him again. "We've got a guy down on Roosevelt Avenue that can take care of these things. But it'll cost you. From now on, when Mr. Marano wants a new piece of equipment, we'll expect it for more than the standard manager's discount. And we'll want to help ourselves to your warehouse from time to time."

Now the dream shifted from memory to the surreal, because as the gangsters were rolling the trash bags over her, Cecelia opened her eyes and spoke to him.

"I'll be back, lover."

Harold screamed, and was still screaming when the phone awoke him. He sat up, bolts of pain going off behind his eyes. He felt funny. Weighted. He fumbled for the phone in the dark.

"Hello?"

"Harold? It's Will."

"What time is it?"

"Umm...nine o'clock. Did I wake you?"

"It's okay. What's up?"

"Well, there're two guys down here. I've seen them in the store before—customers of yours. They say they want a fifty-six inch Magnavox and to put it on the Marano account, but I can't find any record of financing or—"

Harold cut him off. "Give them what they want. Set up delivery. I'll take care of it when I come back."

Will said something in reply, but Harold didn't hear it, because the words were drowned out by a voice in his ear.

"Horsy ride, Daddy. Give me a horsy ride."

Harold gasped.

"Harold, what's wrong?"

"I'm alright, Will. Sorry. A spider ran across the bed."

Another voice whispered in the dark. "I have your heart, Harold. Isn't that what you used to tell me?"

"Is there someone else there, Harold? I didn't mean to interrupt."

"Will, I've gotta go."

He hung up, cutting Will off in mid-sentence, and turned on the light.

His wife's face stared back at him from his chest.

"I have your heart," the face on the tumor repeated. The voice was squeaky, but undeniably Marcy's. The tumor had grown to the size of an apple, and now protruded from the area directly above his heart.

Harold grabbed the sheets, noticing again how heavy his hand felt. He glanced down, and his son smiled back at him. The tumor on his hand wore his son's face, and a second one, the size of a toothpick, had begun to sprout from between his fingers. It looked remarkably like a miniature arm. It's tiny fingers waved at him.

"Want to toss the ball around in the backyard, Dad?"

Harold swung his feet to the floor and tried to get out of bed. The pressing weight on his back almost bore him to the floor, and he heard Danielle's voice again, pleading insistently in his ear "Horsy ride, Daddy. Giddy up!"

He crawled on all fours, while his family chattered at him in their cartoon voices. His wife shook her head back and forth, and seemed to stretch. The tumor grew bigger, now covering his breast.

With a sudden terrible clarity, Harold paused, and with his good hand, lifted the waistband of his boxer shorts and peeked inside.

Cecelia grinned back at him from the head of his penis.

"How may I help you?"

The man on the other end of the line was shouting above the clamoring voices in the background.

"My name is Harold Newton! I need to speak to Doctor Rahn!"

"I'm sorry sir, this is Doctor Rahn's answering service. He's unavailable for the evening. Is this an emergency?"

In the background, a child laughed, and the caller screamed in pain.

"Yes, this is a fucking emergency! Tell him we have to cut the tumors out! We've got to remove them!"

"Please calm down, Mr. Newton. What seems to be the trouble?"

The only answer was a long, anguished howl, and more laughter.

"Please hold the line, Mr. Newton. I'll get an emergency operator on the line for you and send help to your location."

"No time! I'll have to do it myself! Please hurry! Tell them—"

The line went dead.

When the paramedics and police arrived, they found Marcy Newton and her children watching television in the living room, along with a woman they identified as a friend of the family, a woman named Cecelia Ramirez. There was no sign of Harold, and when the police returned the next day for further questioning, the family and the Ramirez woman had vanished as well.

STORY NOTES

I wrote this for an anthology about murderous families. The editor requested a story in which one family member killed another. Unfortunately, the anthology project never came to pass, and, as I said in the story notes for The Cage, *I instead published this in my long out-of-print short story collection* Fear of Gravity. *As an early tale, this was the first time I used the plot device of someone murdering their loved ones, but it's a theme I returned to years later in a short story called* "Bunnies In August" *(which can be found in Deadite Press's edition of* Tequila's Sunrise*). Both stories were distinctly uncomfortable to write, which is one of the hazards of writing horror fiction for a living, I guess.*

The characters of Tony and Vince, their mysterious boss Mr. Marano, and the "guy down on Roosevelt Avenue" have only a small walk-on roll in this tale, but they've had much bigger parts in several of my other works, particularly the novels Clickers 2 *and* Clickers 3 *(both co-written with J.F. Gonzalez), and the short stories* "The Siqqusim Who Stole Christmas" *and* "Crazy For You" *(the latter of which was co-written with Mike Oliveri).*

Speaking of old stories, here's one from the vaults...

LEST YE BECOME

There was something wrong with the back of her head.

The screams were distant now, buzzing in the back of Jack's conscious like mosquitoes. The ringing in his ears drowned out the world. Behind the ringing, his pulse pounded out an erratic beat. The echo of the shotgun still reverberated around the classroom.

Again and again. Two more times in quick succession. *That's not an echo*, Jack thought. *Nick is still shooting.*

Something was wrong with the back of Gina's head. Cradling her in his arms, Jack tried to fight the safe, comforting confusion settling over him and figure it out. Her long, honey-blonde hair was crimson now. He didn't like what she'd done with it. Why would she change it without letting him know? They were married. Shouldn't she want his opinion? He winced when he touched it. His hand came away sticky, like tree sap.

Another shot from behind him, then one more.

On Gina's desk, was a picture of the two of them at Niagara Falls. There was his proof. Her hair wasn't red in their honeymoon picture. Just two smiling people. Happy. In love. Next to the picture frame was a half-eaten stick of celery and a ceramic salt shaker with "World's Greatest Teacher" emblazoned on it. Fragments of a shattered coffee mug lay scattered across the desk, marking the passage of a shotgun slug on its way to meet his wife.

Jack gazed back down at Gina, shaking her lightly in his arms. *Not too hard,* he cautioned himself. *After all, she is pregnant.* He desperately wanted her to wake up so they could escape. He needed to get her and the baby both to safety.

There were sirens outside now, and somebody moaned from the hallway. Through the ceiling, he heard the heavy thrum of a helicopter.

Jack turned his attention back to his wife. Greenish-gray pulpy things were splattered across the chalkboard where she'd been standing when he'd chased Nick into the classroom. He didn't want to look at those. He was afraid that they might belong to...

Jack howled, remembering.

Jack gently laid Gina on the floor and turned, timidly peering out from behind the desk. Nick was near the back of the room, walking down the next row. Only a few of the kids were actually screaming. Many more sat in an emotionless state of calm, gazing at Nick with cold, unfeeling eyes. Peggy Lemon glared at him from the floor. Nick placed the barrel of the shotgun against her head and pulled the trigger.

Jack winced, shutting his eyes again as bits of Peggy ran down the wall. The image burned itself into his brain. Blood and more of that same greenish-gray material. *Could that be right?* He wondered. *Brains aren't green, are they?*

Glenn Rutherford chose that moment to make a dash for the door. In one fluid movement, Nick spun and fired into his back. Glenn stumbled a few more feet before crashing to the floor. The screaming continued.

"Shit," Nick said to the room, walking on down the aisle. "He wasn't one of you. See what you things made me do?"

He paused, glancing at Teri Johnson, and then moved on to Justin Miller. Justin, who had won every fist fight he'd ever been in since the second grade, sobbed loudly and held his copy of MOBY DICK up in front of his face with trembling hands.

"Don't even front, mother-fucker," Nick said. "You're not Justin."

Immediately, the frightened pleas ceased. Lowering the book, Justin glared at him from over the top of the cover, and then threw back his head and emitted a high-pitched, shrill cry, full of anger and contempt. Another blast, and both the book and the flesh behind it disintegrated.

Jack stepped out from behind Gina's desk as Nick poked Eddie Blumenthal with the barrel of the shotgun. A dark stain appeared on the front of Eddie's jeans and he began to whimper.

"Nick," Jack pleaded. "Don't do this! Just don't..."

"Are those real tears?" Nick spoke softly, as if to himself. Using the shotgun, Nick motioned for Eddie to leave. At that moment, star quarterback Ryan Hadley emitted a horrible shriek identical to the one Justin had made, and bore down on Nick. The young man pulled the trigger and a hole erupted in the football player's mid-section. Ryan stared down at it calmly, his expression passive. Then he grasped for the weapon while Eddie dashed into the hall.

"They're not human," Nick shouted. "But bullets kill them. Salt and bullets."

Nick wrested the shotgun away from Ryan and fired. Ryan's head exploded.

Nick glanced back at Jack. "Salt and bullets, Mr. Madison. You've gotta believe me."

"I believe you, Nick." Jack crept toward the gunman. "I believe you. They hurt you, picked on you. Just put the gun down."

"This isn't about them fucking with me," Nick yelled. "They aren't us! Listen, Mr. Madison. Peggy, Justin, Ryan, my parents, your wife, *none of them are who we think they are!*"

Nick placed the shotgun on an empty desk and cocked his head as if listening for something. Then he looked out the window. The room was quiet now. Jack followed his gaze and frowned at what he saw. There should have been panicked kids streaming out the doors to the safety of the police barricade. Instead, they walked calmly in a slow, straight line. There were no news vans or hordes of reporters and camera crews milling about. Even the police and S.W.A.T. team behaved irrationally, going about their business with an almost lackadaisical demeanor, as if it was a normal day.

Jack stepped back, brushing up against the chalkboard. Something warm and wet seeped through the back of his shirt. He realized that it was his wife's blood. But the sticky liquid felt *wrong* somehow. His vision went blurry. He closed his eyes and listened. His own classroom across the hall was silent. So were most of the kids in this classroom. He opened his eyes again, studying them, disturbed by how they sat quietly. Why weren't they making a break for the door now that Nick's attention was occupied with the window? Jack swallowed hard. His tongue felt swollen and dry in his parched mouth.

"Nick, what is it that you want?"

"I want you to fucking listen to me, Mr. Madison. I want you to help me before it's too late!"

Jack nodded dumbly, aware of just how precarious the situation had grown and how helpless he was to do anything about it.

"First it was my sister," Nick said. "She came back from college out in Los Angeles and she wasn't the same. Then my parents. I started seeing them everywhere! Qwik-Burger, the mall, even online and on television."

Outside, a Kevlar-armored S.W.A.T. member stepped out calmly from behind the barricade and strolled towards the main office door. Nick was staring at the floor and hadn't noticed.

"They're like slugs," Nick said. "I'm not sure how it works, but they get inside your head."

Jack realized that the other students were staring at both him and Nick with undisguised loathing. The cop had disappeared into the building. Presumably, if this situation followed the laws of television, he would come onto the P.A. system and try to negotiate with Nick. Jack calculated his options while Nick babbled. Did he dare to distract Nick, possibly even scuffle with him, to allow the kids a chance to escape? And if he did, would they take the opportunity? They appeared to be in the grip of some bizarre shock; emotionless and uncaring.

Suddenly, each of them erupted with another ear-piercing wail, pointing their fingers at the gunman. Outside, the police stirred behind the barricade. They stood watching in mute silence, the rescued students side-by-side with them, all staring at the classroom windows. Nick grabbed the shotgun, pointed it at his nearest classmate, and pulled the trigger. Nothing happened.

"Empty," he yelled above the din. "You've gotta believe me, Mr. Madison. They're not human!"

The shrieking chorus grew louder. Nick charged around the room, screaming at the students to shut up. Jack's head began to throb. He covered his ears with his hands. Nick thumbed the power button on the classroom television, cranking the volume as loud as it would go, trying to silence the chorus while he fumbled for more shotgun shells.

"Authorities indicate that martial law has been lifted on most of the West Coast, and that the situation is now firmly under control. The public unrest that has gripped the area for the last two weeks has ended, after National Guardsmen were deployed into San Francisco, San Diego, Los Angeles, Portland and Seattle. Coming up, the health benefits of kelp and why you should try it for yourself."

"Do you see?" Nick pointed at the television. "Why isn't there anything about this on the news? Some kid goes nuts in New York and shoots up a High School, and they're talking about fucking *kelp*? They've taken over! They're the real monsters. Not me."

Jack pondered that as more police walked in a leisurely line towards the school. He thought about monsters. Was Nick a monster? Nick, a thin and quiet young man. Nick, a reclusive but highly productive student. Nick, a raving lunatic who had just slain over thirty members of the faculty and student body. Nick who had just killed Jack's wife…

Jack trembled as thoughts of Gina crept back into his consciousness. They had argued last night. She'd been distant and indifferent lately. They hadn't made love since she'd gotten pregnant and he wanted to know if it was something he'd done. Unrelenting, Gina had insisted there was nothing wrong and then rebuffed his tentative advances. Fuming, Jack had slept on the couch. She had been cold to him this morning. Jack had thought she was still mad and chided himself, realizing that her drastic shift in mood was probably due to the hormonal changes going on inside her.

The intercom crackled, and Nick shut off the television. The students stopped shrieking. Jack listened for the rational voice that would try to reason with the gunman, and braced himself for whatever Nick's reaction would be. But instead, something else came from the speakers. Something that was not a language. At least not a language Jack had ever heard before. It was vaguely male, but there was something sexless in the tone. Rather than speech, it delivered a series of dry, clicking sounds. The students listened intently.

Finished reloading, Nick pulled the trigger again and Laura Elkin's face imploded, spraying the peculiar gray and green blood all over the student behind her. Without thinking, Jack charged Nick. Whirling around, Nick leveled the gun at Jack's chest. He hesitated, indecisive, and then Jack was upon him, struggling with the wiry teen. The weapon flew from Nick's grasp and soared across the room, striking the desktop. The gun discharged again. The slug scored the mahogany and sent Gina's ceramic salt shaker flying. Salt rained down on two of the students in the front row, and immediately they began to shriek again.

Jack and Nick broke away from one another, clapping their hands over their ears. The two screeching teens twitched on the floor. White froth bubbled from their noses, mouths, and eyes. Jack stared in horror, whimpering as something small and gray crawled from their ears and began dissolving in a pool of slime. Suddenly, the window exploded, showering the floor with tiny glass daggers.

And then there was silence.

Nick stood gaping, a crimson stain spreading on his shirt.

"Listen," he gasped. "You're next, Mr. Madison. Fight them for me."

Nick staggered two steps toward him. Jack felt the bile, mixed with a sob, rising in his throat. The police sniper fired a second shot and Nick collapsed to the floor.

As the echo of the gunshot faded, Jack finally understood what was wrong with Gina's head.

It wasn't her head anymore.

The bottom fell out of Jack Madison's world. The thing that was not his wife lay still, but her abdomen was *moving*, tiny clicking noises emanating from within her womb.

The remaining students approached him. Jack backed away. He ducked down and picked up the shotgun and fished some more shells from the dead teen's pocket.

His laughter sounded like a scream when he fired the first shot.

STORY NOTES

This is a very old story—one of the first stories I ever had published, in fact. It's not very good (at least, in my opinion), but it's one fans have asked me to have reprinted over the years. Your wish is my command. I resisted the urge to heavily revise it for its inclusion here. It first appeared in an anthology called Poddities, *which was a collection of stories inspired by Jack Finney's* Invasion of the Body Snatchers. *The story was then reprinted in my first collection,* No Rest For the Wicked. *Both books have been out of print for many years now.* Poddities, *edited by Suzanne Donahue, also contained early work by writers such as Nicholas Kaufmann, Tim Lebbon, Christopher Golden, Dan Keohane, and Jeffrey Thomas, as well as work from veteran writers such as Michael Marshall Smith, Ramsey Campbell, Jack Ketchum, Thomas Monteleone, David Silva, and many others. It was an important sale for me, and so, this story has always held a special place in my heart (despite its flaws). I hope you enjoyed it, too. If not, here's one more story that maybe you'll like instead.*

WAITING FOR

FOR

DARKNESS

Trying not to cry, Artie waited.

His older sister, Betty, had buried him up to his head in the sand. He'd been reluctant, but Artie feared her disapproval more than being buried. Betty liked to tease him sometimes. The sand had been warm, at first. Now it was cold. His skin felt hot. His lips were cracked. Blistered. His throat was sore. When he tried to call for help, all that came out was a weak, sputtering sigh. Not that anyone would come, even if he could shout. It was the off season, and the private beach had been deserted all day. Just him and Betty.

And the men.

They'd appeared while Artie pleaded with Betty to free him. Their shadows were long. Betty's laughter died. The men didn't speak. Didn't smile. Just walked right up and punched Betty in the face. Again and again, until she bled.

Then they carried her away.

Artie licked the film of snot coating his upper lip. Gnats flitted around his face. A small crab scuttled near his ear, waving its claws in agitation.

The sun disappeared beneath the ocean. The waves grew dark. Black.

Artie watched the darkness creep closer.

It was very loud.

STORY NOTES

Cemetery Dance Publications asked me to write a story short enough to fit onto a t-shirt. This was it, and it was indeed printed on a line of t-shirts. I was re-reading a lot of Richard Laymon at the time, and I think his influence is very apparent in this tale. In addition to its appearance on a t-shirt, this story also appeared in my now out-of-print short story collection A Conspiracy of One.

BRIAN KEENE is the author of over twenty-five books, including *Darkness on the Edge of Town, Urban Gothic, Castaways, Kill Whitey, Dark Hollow, Dead Sea, Ghoul* and *The Rising*. He also writes comic books such as *The Last Zombie, Doom Patrol* and *Dead of Night: Devil Slayer*. His work has been translated into German, Spanish, Polish, Italian, French and Taiwanese. Several of his novels and stories have been optioned for film, one of which, *The Ties That Bind*, premiered on DVD in 2009 as a critically-acclaimed independent short. Keene's work has been praised in such diverse places as *The New York Times*, The History Channel, The Howard Stern Show, CNN.com, *Publisher's Weekly, Fangoria Magazine*, and *Rue Morgue Magazine*. Keene lives in Central Pennsylvania. You can communicate with him online at www.briankeene.com, on Facebook at www.facebook.com/pages/Brian-Keene/189077221397 or on Twitter at www.twitter.com/BrianKeene

deadite press

"Brain Cheese Buffet" Edward Lee - collecting nine of Lee's most sought after tales of violence and body fluids. Featuring the Stoker nominated "Mr. Torso," the legendary gross-out piece "The Dritiphilist," the notorious "The McCrath Model SS40-C, Series S," and six more stories to test your gag reflex.

"Edward Lee's writing is fast and mean as a chain saw revved to full-tilt boogie."
    - Jack Ketchum

"Bullet Through Your Face" Edward Lee - No writer is more extreme, perverted, or gross than Edward Lee. His world is one of psychopathic redneck rapists, sex addicted demons, and semen stealing aliens. Brace yourself, the king of splatterspunk is guaranteed to shock, offend, and make you laugh until you vomit.
"Lee pulls no punches."
    - Fangoria

"Like Porno for Psychos" Wrath James White - From a world-ending orgy to home liposuction. From the hidden desires of politicians to a woman with a fetish for lions. This is a place where necrophilia, self-mutilation, and murder are all roads to love.

Like Porno for Psychos collects the most extreme erotic horror from the celebrated hardcore horror master. Wrath James White is your guide through sex, death, and the darkest desires of the heart.

"Trolley No. 1852" Edward Lee - In 1934, horror writer H.P. Lovecraft is invited to write a story for a subversive underground magazine, all on the condition that a pseudonym will be used. The pay is lofty, and God knows, Lovecraft needs the money. There's just one catch. It has to be a pornographic story . . . The 1852 Club is a bordello unlike any other. Its women are the most beautiful and they will do anything. But there is something else going on at this sex club. In the back rooms monsters are performing vile acts on each other and doors to other dimensions are opening . . .

deadite press

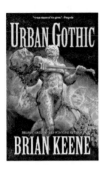

"Urban Gothic" Brian Keene - When their car broke down in a dangerous inner-city neighborhood, Kerri and her friends thought they would find shelter inside an old, dark row home. They thought they would be safe there until help arrived. They were wrong. The residents who live down in the cellar and the tunnels beneath the city are far more dangerous than the streets outside, and they have a very special way of dealing with trespassers. Trapped in a world of darkness, populated by obscene abominations, they will have to fight back if they ever want to see the sun again.

"Ghoul" Brian Keene - There is something in the local cemetery that comes out at night. Something that is unearthing corpses and killing people. It's the summer of 1984 and Timmy and his friends are looking forward to no school, comic books, and adventure. But instead they will be fighting for their lives. The ghoul has smelled their blood and it is after them. But that's not the only monster they will face this summer . . . From award-winning horror master Brian Keene comes a novel of monsters, murder, and the loss of innocence.

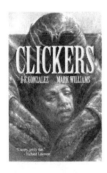

"Clickers" J. F. Gonzalez and Mark Williams- They are the Clickers, giant venomous blood-thirsty crabs from the depths of the sea. The only warning to their rampage of dismemberment and death is the terrible clicking of their claws. But these monsters aren't merely here to ravage and pillage. They are being driven onto land by fear. Something is hunting the Clickers. Something ancient and without mercy. *Clickers* is J. F. Gonzalez and Mark Williams' gore-soaked cult classic tribute to the giant monster B-movies of yesteryear.

"Clickers II" J. F. Gonzalez and Brian Keene- Thousands of Clickers swarm across the entire nation and march inland, slaughtering anyone and anything they come across. But this time the Clickers aren't blindly rushing onto land - they are being led by an intelligence older than civilization itself. A force that wants to take dry land away from the mammals. Those left alive soon realize that they must do everything and anything they can to protect humanity – no matter the cost. *This isn't war, this is extermination.*

"The Book of a Thousand Sins" Wrath James White - Welcome to a world of Zombie nymphomaniacs, psychopathic deities, voodoo surgery, and murderous priests. Where mutilation sex clubs are in vogue and torture machines are sex toys. No one makes it out alive – not even God himself.

"If Wrath James White doesn't make you cringe, you must be riding in the wrong end of a hearse."
-Jack Ketchum

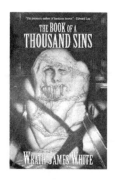

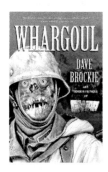

"Whargoul" Dave Brockie - It is a beast born in bullets and shrapnel, feeding off of pain, misery, and hard drugs. Cursed to wander the Earth without the hope of death, it is reborn again and again to spread the gospel of hate, abuse, and genocide. But what if it's not the only monster out there? What if there's something worse? From Dave Brockie, the twisted genius behind GWAR, comes a novel about the darkest days of the twentieth century.

"Take the Long Way Home" Brian Keene - All across the world, people suddenly vanish in the blink of an eye. Gone. Steve, Charlie and Frank were just trying to get home when it happened. Trapped in the ultimate traffic jam, they watch as civilization collapses, claiming the souls of those around them. God has called his faithful home, but the invitations for Steve, Charlie and Frank got lost. Now they must set off on foot through a nightmarish post-apocalyptic landscape in search of answers. In search of God. In search of their loved ones. And in search of home.

"Baby's First Book of Seriously Fucked-Up Shit" Robert Devereaux - From an orgy between God, Satan, Adam and Eve to beauty pageants for fetuses. From a giant human-absorbing tongue to a place where God is in the eyes of the psychopathic. This is a party at the furthest limits of human decency and cruelty. Robert Devereaux is your host but watch out, he's spiked the punch with drugs, sex, and dismemberment. Deadite Press is proud to present nine stories of the strange, the gross, and the just plain fucked up.

THE VERY BEST IN CULT HORROR

deadite press

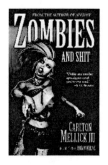

"Zombies and Shit" Carlton Mellick III - Twenty people wake to find themselves in a boarded-up building in the middle of the zombie wasteland. They soon discover they have been chosen as contestants on a popular reality show called Zombie Survival. Each contestant is given a backpack of supplies and a unique weapon. Their goal: be the first to make it through the zombie-plagued city to the pickup zone alive. But because there's only one seat available on the helicopter, the contestants not only have to fight against the hordes of the living dead, they must also fight each other.

"Jack's Magic Beans" Brian Keene - It happens in a split-second. One moment, customers are happily shopping in the Save-A-Lot grocery store. The next instant, they are transformed into bloodthirsty psychotics, interested only in slaughtering one another and committing unimaginably atrocious and frenzied acts of violent depravity. Deadite Press is proud to bring one of Brian Keene's bleakest and most violent novellas back into print once more. This edition also includes four bonus short stories:

"Just Like Hell" Nate Southard- Dillion is a popular high school football star, gay, and tied to a chair in the dark. His lover is bound and gagged next to him. Around him are his teammates -- his captors. They aren't happy that they've been playing with a "faggot" and they intend to repay the disgrace. There will be humiliation, blood, and pain. But then it gets out of control. What started as black-hearted entertainment has turned into a cat-and-mouse game of gruesome justice. By the end of this night, four people will be dead. And those left alive will be forever scared.

"Depraved" Bryan Smith - Welcome to Hopkins Bend. You're never getting out of here alive... In the middle-of-nowhere, USA, there is a town not on any map. A place where outsiders are tortured, raped, and eaten. Where local law enforcement runs a sex trafficking ring. And the woods hold even more monstrous secrets. Today four unlucky travelers will end up in Hopkins Bend. If they want to ever get out alive they will have to become just as vicious and violent as their pursuers. Just as depraved.

Horror That'll Carve a Smile on Your Face.

CUT CORNERS VOLUME 1
Ramsey Campbell, Bentley Little, & Ray Garton

Peel your eyes open, get comfortable, and let three of the horror genre's hardest hitters take you for a ride. Prepare yourselves, my friends, for you are placing your sanity in the hands of these masters of the macabre.

Three brand new stories guaranteed to slice open a smile.

SACRIFICE
Wrath James White

All over town, little girls are going missing and turning up starved, dehydrated, and nearly catatonic. One man is eaten alive by his own dog along with half the pets in the neighborhood. An elementary school teacher is beaten to death by his own students while being stung by thousands of bees. It's up to Detective John Malloy and his partner Detective Mohammed Rafik to figure out how it's all connected to a mysterious voodoo priestess with the power to take away all of your hatred ... all of your fear ... all of your pain.

THE KILLINGS
J.F. Gonzalez & Wrath James White

In 1911, Atlanta's African American community was terrorized by a serial killer that preyed on young bi-racial women, cutting their throats and mutilating their corpses. In the 1980s, more than twenty African American boys were murdered throughout Atlanta. In 2011, another string of sadistic murders have begun, and this time it's more brutal than ever. If Carmen Mendoza, an investigative reporter working for Atlanta's oldest newspaper, can solve the murders, she may find the key to ending the violent curse gripping Atlanta's Black community. If not, she might just become the next victim.

WWW.SINISTERGRINPRESS.COM

CPSIA information can be obtained at www.ICGtesting.com
Printed in the USA
BVOW011309110512

290002BV00011B/29/P

9 781621 050216